The Island Expats Book 2
(Bondu and Beyond)
By Deb McEwan

Cover Design by Jessica Bell

In loving memory of
Samuel Maurice Masters
20 October 1922 to 26 December 2020
Gone but not forgotten.

The Island Expat series is set on the fictional island of Souvia, shown on the map above (capital Souva).

Photographs of the countryside known as bondu to
Souvians.

Chapter 1

It was quiet at the airport when Matt and Keith arrived for Matt's early morning flight. With his bags checked in, and ready to board the plane, the two men turned to face each other. Although neither were looking forward to saying goodbye, Matt couldn't wait to see Elena again and was excited to be moving to Souvia.

'See you, mate, and don't worry, I'll look after everything here for you,' Keith told Matt before enveloping him in a tight man hug.

'I'm struggling to breathe here,' Matt said, pulling himself away from his good friend. 'I'm only a flight away and we'll speak every week on Teams. It's not like we won't see each other again.'

'I know, but it's the end of an era.'

'And the start of a new chapter of my life, as they say.'

'I know it's going to be fine with you and Elena, and the business, Matt, especially if you can get some work over there. It's ticking along nicely here, and I've already spoken to Dale about working on the missing Filipino women.'

'That's going to take ages to unravel. Looks like the traffickers work in a number of countries,' Matt answered. 'Can you imagine? The evil of some people still amazes me, even after everything I've seen.'

'Me too, Matt, and I'd worry if it didn't.'

'But I'm still planning on settling in with Elena first, and am going to concentrate on getting Jenny and myself sorted while we get used to living with somebody else again. The business can wait.'

Keith didn't believe it for a minute, but wasn't going to argue. 'You don't intend to look for any new work for a while then?' he asked. They'd already discussed this, but he was fishing to see whether Matt had changed his mind.

Matt knew exactly what Keith was up to and the men smiled at each other. 'The business started out as just a pastime, Keith, something to…' He didn't finish the sentence but they both knew that Matt's business had been a distraction for him to keep sane and to have something to focus on through the worst of his PTSD.

'If you weren't so stubborn and bloody-minded…' Keith started, wondering for a brief moment what would have happened if Matt's condition had worsened or if he hadn't accepted the fact that he needed help. 'Anyway, that's all behind you now and—'

'It'll never be behind me, Keith. I know the signs and what to do when… when the horrors... when it happens. Anyway, this isn't—'

'Does Elena know?'

'Elena knows I was on the train when it crashed and that I have nightmares because of it. And she still wants to be with me.' Matt smiled. 'Why the hell are we talking about this in the middle of the airport? I have a flight to catch otherwise Jenny will think she's been abandoned again if she wakes up in Vouni and I'm not there.' Matt held out his hand for a final shake but changed his mind. He gave Keith one last hug. 'Thanks for sticking by me, mate, and we'll speak once I'm settled in. Yes?'

'Will do, Matt, or should I say, sounds like a—'

'Bye, Keith. Look after yourself.' Matt picked up his bag and began to make his way to the departure lounge.

'You too, mate,' Keith called after him.

Matt acknowledged this with a wave of his hand, having no idea of the gruesome surprise that was in store for him later that day.

Chapter 2

The flight was uneventful and, three and a half hours after taking off, touched down in Vouni, Souvia's second city and the main airport for the tourist trade on the Western side of the island.

Matt cleared customs and collected his luggage then was asked to wait in a holding area while the airport vet carried out the required checks on his dog Jenny. Almost thirty minutes later, a young woman came to find him.

'Mr Elliott?'

'Yes,' Matt replied, even though he was the only one in the room.

'You have a very lively dog waiting for you. Come with me please.'

Matt followed the woman outside. He stepped into her small van and she drove around the back of the main airport area where there were a number of other buildings of assorted sizes, one with the words *Vouni Airport Veterinary Services* painted on the wall next to the door. *Does what it says on the box,* Matt raised an eyebrow at the unimaginative title.

They heard dogs barking as they approached the building, and he followed the woman inside and through to the back. There was a door with a glass panel at head height and he looked through it straight to the outside areas where he could see individual, enclosed, artificially grassed pens with borders filled with earth. Jenny was in the zone straight ahead, sniffing where the earth was before squatting for a pee.

'She seems to have calmed down now,' the woman said, as she opened the door.

Jenny looked up at the sound and saw Matt. She spun around in a circle three times and her tail looked as if it had a mind of its own as that, too, spun like an out-of-control propeller.

'I take it back,' the woman said, laughing as they walked outside.

Jenny ran at Matt and jumped. He saw what was going to happen and readied himself. As he caught her in his arms, the momentum made him take a step back but he managed to stay upright. She covered his face in big licks and Matt was caught up in her enthusiasm.

'I love you too, but it's only been eight hours, not three months!' He put Jenny on the floor and bent down to give her all the attention she deserved.

The woman looked on indulgently and gave them a few moments before speaking. 'I have some papers for you to sign,' she said. 'I'll go and get them. I don't think Jenny would be too amused if you left her again.' She laughed and went back through the door.

In a hurry to see the two-legged love of his life, Matt signed the papers and then he and Jenny got back into the van and the woman drove through to the airport exit gate where she stopped to let her passengers out.

He received a few stares as he lifted the heavy rucksack onto his back, wheeled the case behind him with his right hand and held Jenny's lead in the other. The dog was uncomfortable in crowded places and Matt could tell she was nervous from the way her tail hung down and her head moved from side to side, as though she were trying to look for an escape route. He looked for somewhere suitable and encouraged Jenny over to an empty bus shelter, put his case to one side and sat down on the bench so that he could soothe the sweet girl.

'It's all right, Jenny,' he said. 'There's nothing to be afraid of. Nobody's going to hurt you. Come on, let's go and meet Elena.'

A few people walking by looked at the man talking to his dog and shook their heads, not understanding the bond between them. Others smiled indulgently and one of those was almost beside herself with excitement as she waited as patiently as she could. But the anticipation was too much for her— at the same time as Jenny looked up and woofed a gentle bark, Elena said a quiet, 'Hello, Matt.'

He'd been totally absorbed by Jenny and her voice took him by surprise. 'Elena!' he said, jumping up and grabbing her. He lifted her up and then swung her around.

Elena giggled like a schoolgirl until Matt stopped and put her down. 'Elena,' he said again as he looked at her, and then, oblivious to anyone in the vicinity, they kissed. Not even Jenny pawing Matt's leg stopped them, but when she jumped up and tried to get in between them, they broke apart.

'Hello. You must be Jenny?' Elena said, as she bent and stroked the dog. Jenny kept nudging Elena for more attention to which her new people parent obliged, until Matt interrupted.

'As lovely as it is to watch you both, can we get on before it gets dark?'

With the two-hour time difference and Matt's six am flight, it was only a little after twelve thirty. Elena smiled at Matt's sarcastic comment.

'The car's in the car park, a few minutes' walk,' Elena said, taking the dog's lead while Matt hoisted the

6

rucksack onto his back and dragged his suitcase behind him.

'Lead the way,' he said.

The novelty of being led by the new person was enough for Jenny to forget her jitters for a few minutes as they walked to the car park. Matt went to put his bags in the boot of the SUV, but stopped when he saw the dog bed.

'She usually rides in the back of the car,' he said, 'not the boot.'

'Can we start as we mean to go on, please Matt? Then Jenny won't know any different from the off. She can still lean over to the back seat, but it'll confine most of her hairs to the boot this way, and won't do her any harm. Look,' Elena added with a laugh, as Jenny looked from one to the other of the people who were talking about her.

'Up, Jenny,' Matt said. She looked at him once again in silent protest, and Matt had to repeat himself before Jenny jumped into the boot and turned around in the dog bed a few times, before eventually plonking herself down with a sigh.

'Good girl,' Elena said, giving the dog an affectionate pat. Jenny's tail thumped gently.

'I'll sit in the back,' Matt said, and Elena rolled her eyes. 'Everything's new to her so just to make sure she's not freaked out.'

Elena shrugged her shoulders and got into the driving seat.

Matt had rented a three-bedroom house in Oristos, the one he'd taken Elena to see on his last day in Souvia, two months earlier. She had already been living in a smaller house in the town and they agreed it was the

7

perfect house to start their new life together. Elena started the car and pulled out into the traffic, beginning their journey home.

Five minutes into the drive, Matt felt like a plonker and asked Elena to pull over. 'I'm being over-protective and I was wrong,' he said, moving from the back to the front passenger seat. 'I'll try to get with the programme, I promise.'

'And I'll try to be patient, but it's not a problem, Matt. It's going to take Jenny a little while to get used to her new surroundings and the living arrangements. And us too. It's been years since I've lived with anyone or had to look after anyone other than myself.'

'Me too, Elena, and I'm here to look after you,' he said. 'Or to spoil you, at the very least,' he added when he saw the look on her face.

'I can do spoiled, Matt. My ex-husband said he wanted to look after me but that meant controlling my every move. Sorry, that was some time ago and I know you're nothing like my ex, but it had such a profound effect on me that I still think about it from time to time.'

'This is a big step for us both, Elena, and you're right, I'm nothing like your ex. I have my skeletons too, but I'm sure we'll be fine.'

'Me too. But let's agree to be honest and to tell each other if something isn't right.'

'I can't imagine you being anything else, Elena. This is the best I've felt in ages and I'm just glad to be here with you.'

'Me too, Matt. Now let's get our new little family settled into our new home.'

She pulled onto the highway and they chatted about their plans for the next few days as Elena had taken time off work. A family dinner was on the cards for the end of the following week but they intended to keep themselves to themselves for the first week.

'We can talk about whatever changes you want to make in the house and then we can relax at the beach, check out the tourist sites, the local bars and restaurants or just chill at home. Whatever you want to do, Matt. As long as we're together, I don't really care.'

'Me neither.' He squeezed her hand and looked at her face, hardly believing how fortunate he was that this woman loved him as much as he loved her.

Exiting the highway a few minutes after the Griffon Point exit, Elena drove down into the valley between Griffon Point and Oristos. This part of the journey always reminded Matt of the start of a roller coaster ride, from the dip to the steep incline, such was the feel of the hill. Exiting the road into the small town, she drove down another dip, then up again and took a left into the town. They passed a few shops, bars and restaurants on what the townies referred to as the strip, and arrived at their new home, on the outskirts at the other side of the town. It was only a short walk to two small, family-run restaurants, a corner shop that sold almost everything and a café-come-bar no bigger than the average front room. Five old men were sitting at a table outside the café, and they waved as Elena drove past the two detached houses and came to their rental, the penultimate detached house on the street.

Matt took an intake of breath and looked at the beautiful house, hardly believing he was going to live there with the woman and dog that he loved. It was a gem and he was glad he'd found it, especially as he recalled the look on Elena's face when he'd surprised her before leaving the island last time.

The two-storey building was painted white. Matt had fallen in love with the sea view from the balcony of the master bedroom, even though this particular feature made the property more expensive than some of the other properties in Oristos, the majority of which were overlooked. The house was modern with gas central heating – a must, Elena said, in case they had a rare, cold winter and an efficient air conditioning system – another must for the intensely hot summers. There was plenty of outside space with a decent sized pool – which would be great for summers and entertaining, and two of the three bedrooms had en suite bathrooms. Matt got the message when Elena told him this was a must for any visiting guests.

'Home, sweet home,' she said, opening the front door with a flourish, her eyes shining with happiness.

Matt quickly fed Jenny and let her explore the outside of the property after she'd had a good wander and sniff around the inside. Elena had thoughtfully arranged for astro-turf to be laid with the permission of the owners, so Jenny had dog-friendly places to run around in the low-maintenance garden. Impatient to spend some time alone with Elena without worrying about the dog, he called her back in after she'd done her business and she plonked herself down in her bed, set between the two and three-seat sofas.

'I'll show you what else I've done,' Elena said.

'Not just yet,' Matt said, turning to her and sweeping her into his arms. She got the message. They disappeared upstairs into the master bedroom and the dog sighed and waited for them to come out.

10

Some thirty minutes later, Elena ran her hand down Matt's cheek and smiled. 'Welcome home.' He answered her with a long, deep kiss. 'I think I'll have a shower and unpack.'

'Good idea, and I'll make us a quick bite to eat after I've showered.'

Matt opened the bedroom door. Jenny heard and ran up the stairs and straight into the room. She ran first to Matt for reassurance, then around to Elena's side of the bed. Elena stroked and cuddled her and Jenny lapped it up.

'Don't think you're sleeping on the bed, young lady,' Elena said, as the dog pawed her for more attention.

They had a light meal of Elena's home-made vegetable soup with fresh rolls from the bakery and Matt delayed his unpacking, enjoying sitting with Elena and shooting the breeze. It was approaching four o'clock by the time he'd finished his unpacking, and realised that Jenny was sitting in front of him trying to convey that she wanted something by staring at Matt.

'I'll take Jenny out for a long walk over the bondu and then we can decide where to go for dinner tonight. Coming?'

'But of course, Matt. We'll eat out tonight—on the strip if you like?'

A few minutes later they were ready to explore the countryside around their new home.

'I think we'll go this way to the bondu,' Elena said, pointing to the left, 'rather than through the paved streets. The countryside will be more interesting for Jenny and she can explore all the bushes and sniff at the trees. The views are stunning too, Matt. Though some of the countryside around us can be a little beige in the

11

height of summer, there's plenty of green at this time of year and with no houses to block our view, we can see clearly all the way to the sea.'

Matt had Jenny's lead in his right hand and took Elena's hand in his left as they headed for the bondu. 'What time's sunset?' he asked.

'About five thirty today, well that's what it says on my phone. We'll be back before it gets dark though. We'll need to keep our eyes open as it's been a mild winter and there's been some reports of snakes. Unusual at this time of year.'

'Snakes?' Matt asked, stopping to look at Elena.

Elena laughed at the horror on his face. 'Yes, Matt, snakes. 'The blunt nosed-viper is poisonous, but we tend not to get many of those around here. That's what I'm told, anyway. We're more likely to see a whipsnake in this area but these aren't poisonous thankfully, and they kill the vipers, which is good news isn't it?'

'Err, yes,' Matt said, knowing he'd need to keep a careful eye on Jenny. Like most dogs she loved digging in bushes and under stones and if snakes made their homes there…

'Are you all right Matt? Don't look so worried. I'm told we can get something from the vet to inject into Jenny in case of snake poisoning, and that would stop the poison from doing its worst before we could get her to the vet, if this were to happen,' Elena said. She saw the look of dismay on Matt's face and rushed to reassure him. 'It's just a precaution. When I went to see the vet, he told me that he hasn't treated any dogs for snake bites for a number of years. Certainly not from this area anyway.'

'It's a lot to take in, Elena, that's all. I need to get a stick or spear or something so I can kill any before they have a chance to…'

'A spear? Are you off your rocker, Matt? And anyway, most snakes are protected so you can't kill them.'

'What do you mean I can't kill them. If a snake were to come anywhere near Jenny…'

'You'd take Jenny away and then contact Snake Stavros.'

'Snake Stavros?'

'Yup, the island expert. He catches snakes that are occasionally found too close to towns or cities and returns them to their natural environment. He has a collection of exotic snakes too and some other reptiles. Maybe we should visit one day.'

Matt looked at Elena as if she were mad and then shook his head. 'Are you sure we should go walking in the bondu?'

Elena laughed. 'It's fine, honestly. I see people taking their dogs there every day, and letting them off their leads. Come on, don't be a wimp.'

'I'll show you who's a flaming wimp,' he said, trying to grab her with his free hand. Elena dodged it and ran ahead and Matt started to chase her. Jenny had no idea what was going on, but she barked as it seemed like fun.

A few minutes-walk into the bondu, Matt decided to let Jenny off the lead, knowing that if he didn't do it from the off, he would always be over-cautious. Now it was Elena's turn to question.

'Will she be all right?'

'Because of the snakes?'

'No, silly. Does she run away? I mean she doesn't know her way around this area yet and if she was to get too far ahead of us and get lost, it could take ages to find her.'

'She has a herding instinct, Elena, but she's cautious about new areas too. She'll run ahead of us, but not too far, and every so often will run back to check that we're still here. I need to let her off the lead now because if I don't, I'll always be thinking about the snakes. As you said earlier, let's start how we mean to go on.'

Elena smiled and squeezed his hand in answer, and they carried on with their walk.

Deep into the countryside, Matt stopped to listen to the birdsong and to admire the view. At this height above sea level, they could see the coast off into the distance ahead of them and a number of rolling hills and mountains to each side. Although Elena had talked about the view, he hadn't appreciated how breath taking it would be. 'It's absolutely stunning,' he said. 'And I don't think I'll ever tire of this view.'

'Me neither, Matt. This is great therapy after a stressful day at work.'

Jenny's barking broke the mood.

'She only barks to tell me something,' he said as the dog came running towards them. Once she knew she had their attention, she ran forwards, away from them and then doubled back again, repeating the moves a few times, making it obvious that she wanted them to follow. A few paces later, Jenny left the beaten track and started pushing her way through the shrubbery. The deeper in she went the taller it became, and Matt had to part bushes so that he and Elena could make their way through. Jenny became impatient and barked.

'I don't know what's wrong with her,' Matt said, after a questioning look from Elena. 'She's never done anything like this before. At least, not with me, anyway.'

They followed her and a few seconds later they saw bushes that looked like they'd been disturbed. 'It looks like someone's been here before, Matt, and dumped something by the looks of it. Look at that big blue bag. I get fed up with people dumping their rubbish in the countryside, they have no respect for the environment and—' She stopped talking and put her head to one side. 'Oh my God! Matt, is that a *hand*?'

Jenny was now sitting next to the plastic bag which was partially obscured by the bushes. The part they could see had a hole in it. An arm was indeed hanging out of the hole that had been made in the bag. The hand was small and delicate looking, with long, red-painted nails.

'Good girl, Jenny,' Matt said as he took his phone out of his pocket.

'I'll go and—'

'Stay here with me, Elena, please. We don't know how long ago she was dumped here or if anyone else is about.' He lifted the hand and felt for a pulse, but there was nothing. Turning to Elena, Matt shook his head. 'Phone 112 and I'll phone George.'

Elena had already taken her phone out of her pocket to call the emergency services. She told them about the discovery while Matt phoned DCI George Constantinou, Elena's cousin who also happened to be a homicide detective. George was based in Vouni, Souvia's second city and the nearest to Matt and Elena's home.

'It's Matt, George. We're out walking in the bondu and have come across a body inside a plastic bag. Her arm is hanging out of the plastic and all I can tell from

15

that is that she's quite small and maybe in her twenties or thirties at first guess. The hand is quite delicate, but I can't tell anything else without disturbing the body and the scene.'

'Welcome to Souvia, Matt. Did you arrive today?'

'Yes, and I know, this is the second body I've found in Souvia. I'll try not to make a habit of it.'

'I think it's a bit late for that, Matt! We'll be there as soon as we can, but I'll get some uniformed officers...'

'Elena's already made that call, George, so any cars in the area will already be on their way. We're not easy to find.' Matt explained where they were, then they hung up.

Jenny ran back to the bushes and started pulling at the bag, ripping it and exposing one side of the woman's face as she did so.

'No girl,' Matt said, as the dog licked the woman's cheek. 'Leave her alone.' He pulled Jenny back and they waited.

Elena's phone rang ten minutes later, and she gave directions to where they were to the police sergeant on the other end of the phone. They heard the sirens shortly after and a little time passed before uniformed police made it to their location. One of them was police sergeant Demetri Lambrou.

'Well, if it isn't our very own Mr Elliott,' Demetri said, clapping Matt on the back. 'How are you doing, Matt?'

'I was doing fine, Demi, until we came upon this discovery. Jenny must have smelled something and then she led us to the bag, and....'

'Not a very nice discovery at all,' Demetri said. He turned to Elena. 'Are you the one who made the call?'

Elena nodded.

'I need to take a statement guys before the boss arrives. The constables here will cordon off the area. Shall we move back a bit so they can get on with it?'

'Good idea,' Matt said, as they moved away from the scene. 'I called DCI George Constantinou while Elena was on the phone to you and he's already on his way. He was going to call Doctor Kostas and bring him with him if he was free, or Doctor Anna.'

Doctor Kostas was the head of forensics and Doctor Anna his main assistant and Demetri nodded his head in acknowledgement.

'You were walking your dog?'

'That's right,' Matt said. 'We've only arrived today, Demi, but I wanted Jenny to get familiarised with the local area, so Elena suggested the bondu would be good after a long flight.'

'We certainly didn't expect to find...' Elena said, leaving her sentence unfinished as she wondered who the woman in the bag was. 'How could someone do this to another human being? I mean, it's just awful— and what if…' She stopped as she saw the look of concern on the faces of both men.

'It is awful,' Demi said gently, 'and I suggest you get off home as soon as we've finished here.' Demi didn't want Elena to be around when George and the forensic team cut away the bag to examine the contents, and also to see if they could establish the woman's identity.

Whilst Elena and Matt were distracted by talking to the police, Jenny ran back to the body. She now sat by the woman's side and waited.

'Come, Jenny,' Matt said, but she ignored him.

George arrived shortly after, along with Dr Kostas Demetriou and DS Chloe Petrou.

After they said their hellos, George took Matt to one side. 'Another day, another body,' he said. 'But it's good to see you, Matt, despite the gruesome circumstances.'

'You too, George. And it's great to be here, at long last.' Matt said. He looked towards Elena and smiled.

'How is she?'

'It's a shock, but I'll keep an eye on her. She'll be all right.'

'What's with the dog, Matt?' Dr Kostas asked after a quick look towards the scene.

'She tried licking the woman earlier and now she won't move from her unless I drag her away. Sorry, I'll sort it…'

'She may be trying to tell you something,' Kostas said, as they walked towards the woman.

Matt shrugged at George as they both followed. The forensic photographer arrived a matter of seconds later and joined them. He quickly started to take photographs as Dr Kostos watched Matt talking to his dog. The sun was getting lower in the sky and it wouldn't be long before it was completely dark. Dr Kostos knelt on the ground and, wondering if Matt's dog had picked up something that they hadn't, put his fingers on the woman's neck, over her carotid artery.

'Call an ambulance, now,' he said. 'She's alive!'

The atmosphere changed as soon as he'd said the words. DS Chloe made the call and Matt and George followed the instructions of Dr Kostas to get the woman as comfortable as they could before the ambulance arrived. One of the policemen took off his jacket and they covered the woman, whose skin felt cold to the touch.

The blue plastic no longer covered the woman's head and Matt took a step back now that he could see all of her face. Long dark hair framed a small, delicate nose and full lips, and although her eyes were closed, what he saw were other dark brown eyes staring at him. Even in the twilight he knew that she could have been the double of the girl in the train crash and that image of the scene on the train hit him like a ton of bricks.

'Are you all right?' George asked quietly, and Matt knew he had to get a grip.

'I'm fine.' Even to himself, his voice sounded strange.

George's look said that he needed some sort of explanation.

'She looks uncannily like another victim from…' He stopped himself, not wanting to discuss this with George. 'It was a shock but I'm fine.'

George seemed to accept his brief explanation and remained stern-faced as they watched the proceedings. The girl still had pumps on her feet and was dressed in three quarter length leggings and a plain top. Practical gear, maybe for a domestic job, Matt thought, but the top was skewwhiff which also made him wonder if she had dressed herself. Her well-manicured nails would be impractical for a domestic assistant role. She had deep red marks on her neck and the officers assumed the person who had done this, believed they had killed her.

'It seems that your dog knew, Matt,' George said.

'Good girl,' Matt said, absentmindedly, giving Jenny a pat.

'Thoughts?' George asked.

'I wondered if her day job was in somebody's home and she was either very particular with her nails and hands or maybe she had a more exotic job during the nights. Or, someone dressed her in that gear to put us off the scent.'

The ambulance arrived as they talked and the medics went about their work, quickly attaching an IV line and covering her with a blanket and foil to bring her body temperature back up as fast as they could. They then lifted her onto a stretcher and into the back of the vehicle.

'Are you all right to stay for a while if I get one of the constables to take Elena home?' George asked, as they all watched the ambulance drive off, blue lights flashing.

'That's not a very good way for me to look after Elena, is it, George?'

'You're right, but I want to discuss a job with you; and if my hunch is correct, there may be a connection to this woman,' George replied, and his guess that Matt would be too curious to say no was spot on.

'Let me speak to Elena, but as long as it won't take too long.' Matt made his way back to Elena and took her arm, drawing her to one side. He was touched that Elena picked up Jenny's lead so that the dog went with them.

'Your cousin has asked for my help. I can't explain now but would you be okay for one of the police to take you back home, and I'll be there as soon as I've finished?'

'But Matt, it's your first night!'

'I know, Elena. No probs, I'll tell George I can't help. We can catch up tomorrow.'

'No, don't do that. But please, try not to be too long.'

'Of course.'

Jenny seemed quite happy to go with Elena and a little while later they arrived where the collection of police cars was parked. An officer opened a car door for Elena and the dog to get in.

'We're walking,' she said, to the chagrin of the rather overweight constable who sighed, resigned to the fact that he would have to walk with her. He made a token protest.

'But I need to stay with you so I need to bring my car.'

'You can either come into the house or come back and get it. I'm sure the suspects will be long gone, and this one,' she stroked Jenny's head, 'this one will notify me if there are any intruders.'

The officer walked alongside Elena and was pleasantly surprised that it wasn't too far to their house.

Back in the bondu, George, Matt, and Chloe watched from a distance as Dr Kostas, dressed in his overalls, and the forensic photographer did their work. Even though the woman was alive, there was evidence to be collected and they didn't want to miss anything. Dr Kostas talked as he worked, recording everything for posterity, and the forensic photographer worked away, quietly taking photographs from every angle.

George and Matt continued watching for a while, asking questions of Dr Kostas when he made various comments. When the sun finally set, Dr Kostas stood up straight and stretched his back.

'I've finished for now,' he said. 'But we'll need to come back in the morning to check we haven't missed anything in this light, and also to see if there's anything in the surrounding area.'

'No problem, doc,' Chloe said.

Dr Kostas gave George a nod and said goodbye. As the forensic team left, Chloe talked to Demetri who arranged for the scene to be secured overnight, in the unlikely event that the perpetrators would return. They knew it was more likely that nosey townies would come for a look when the word got out.

They made their way out of the bondu, back into the populated part of the town, and George steered Matt out of listening distance of the others, shining his torch to mark their route while they walked along the path together.

'I take it this has something to do with why you want to speak to me?' Matt said.

'And that's why I want your help with something; you do have a sixth sense for these things.'

Matt ignored the flattery and waited.

'It's come to light that a number of women have gone missing. Specifically, women who came here to work as domestic assistants or housekeepers. The number could be bigger than we thought possible and I don't have enough officers to carry out the investigation. I've already spoken to the boss, who likes you, Matt.' He smiled. 'I'd like to offer you a job. It's boring, humdrum work, but key to our investigation, and you can log into the secure system from anywhere so can do your work from home if you so desire. What do you say?'

'Do you think that the girl in the bondu is something to do with the others who are missing?'

'That would be speculation on my part, but yes, that's what my gut instinct tells me.'

Matt had been unable to help the family of the woman on the train. Her image and that of the female in the bondu merged into one and he knew the only way to stop either from haunting him was to tackle it head on. But still… 'I'll need to talk to Elena first and, if I agree, I won't be able to start straight away.'

George raised an eyebrow and bit back his initial response. 'Do that. But let me know as soon as you can.'

'Will do.' They arrived at the house and Jenny came running out to greet them, with Elena bringing up the rear.

'Are you coming in, George?' Elena asked, purely out of politeness.

'It's been a long day for us all,' George said. 'I'll leave you to it and we'll catch up at the weekend as planned.'

Elena hid her relief as they said their goodbyes and they waved George off before entering the house.

Despite having showered earlier, Matt felt like he needed another, hoping to wash the image of the comatose woman out of his system. He certainly had a distraction for a short time when Elena unexpectedly joined him.

Refreshed both inside and out, they dressed and talked about where they would eat. 'Only two of the restaurants aren't dog-friendly,' Elena said. 'An up-market Italian and a local where the owner was attacked by a dog when she was young and is scared of them.'

'You've done your homework.'

'Remember I've lived here for a while, Matt. Come on, Jenny,' she added, turning to the dog.

The steak house meal was tasty, but they were both simply going through the motions. Although happy at being together, neither could shake off the event that had marred their excitement at being together, forever. Elena had a picture of the young woman's hand in her mind,

23

the brightly coloured nail-varnish at the forefront. And as for Matt, the images of the dead girl on the train and the woman in the bondu merged in his mind yet again, and he struggled to separate one from the other. Jenny was perfectly tuned in to Matt and she got up from her lying position on the floor and sat down next to Matt. She put her head on his thigh, sighed, and looked up at him.

'It's all right, girl,' he said. 'We're fine.'

'Good grief,' Elena said. 'She knows that's shaken you up today.'

'I've seen plenty of dead bodies, Elena, and it's not seeing one that we thought was dead that's shaken me up. It's just that…' He stopped and took a deep breath. 'Look, I don't particularly want to talk about this here.' The restaurant was busy and Matt looked around. 'Can we just finish our meal and go home? And yes, Jenny seems to be tuned into my feelings and can tell when something's wrong. If it wasn't for her, who knows how long it would have taken for someone to find the woman. I'm almost certain she wouldn't have lasted the night. Good girl, Jenny,' he added, giving his furry friend some more attention.

Elena waited until he looked up from Jenny, and then she took his hand. 'I know you've had issues, Matt and I'm not forcing anything. We can talk about it or not, no pressure.'

'Thanks, love.'

'There's a bottle of red at home. We can curl up on the sofa and talk or watch a series, or even…?'

'You're going to wear me out, Elena,' he replied, at the same time signalling the waiter to bring the bill. 'I knew our reunion was going to be special but I didn't pencil in the surprise we got today.'

'Well, Matt, you've said before that I can always surprise you, but not even I expected that sort of surprise.' They both laughed before turning serious. 'That poor girl and her poor family. I hope they can find the person who did this to her, and I hope she makes it.'

'Me too, Elena. I'm sure George will do everything in his power to do so, and if I can help him, I certainly will. It's too early to say what her chances of survival are, I think.' Matt forced a smile back onto his face. 'Shall we?' he said, and got up to help Elena out of her chair.

Back at home, Matt decided it was about time that Elena knew the full story of his problem. But they'd had enough for one day and they were both exhausted. Jenny was already fast asleep in her downstairs bed.

'I'm shattered, Matt.'

'Me too,' he said. He'd been up since the small hours to catch the early morning flight and it was now catching up on him. 'Shall we leave the wine until tomorrow and call it a night?'

'Good idea. Come on, Jen,' Elena said and went to the front door, the dog getting up to stretch before following behind her. 'Go and have a pee.'

The dog did as bid and Matt laughed at how quickly Jenny had got into the new routine. 'Anyone would think she'd been living here for months,' he said as she followed them up the stairs and settled into her soft night bed.

They wrapped their arms around each other. 'I love you,' Matt said, 'and I want to spend the rest of my life with you.'

'I love you too, Matt, and ditto. Sleep well and let's hope for a less eventful day tomorrow.'

'Goodnight, darling,' he said, kissing her tenderly before closing his eyes.

Elena sighed contentedly and looked at Matt, exploring his handsome face, and each line that had marked his journey through life. Within a minute he was breathing heavily and she fell asleep shortly after.

Chapter 3

More than two months had passed since the death of her husband. Fiona Green had come to terms with the fact that she was on her own and had to look after herself. She now recalled her affair with Stephen Goodman as if it had been years, and not months, ago and the fact that his ex-girlfriend had killed her husband – although whether she had intended to kill or maim him was for the jury to decide – Fiona knew the media would love the story. *Loved, not would love,* she corrected herself mentally as she recalled the hounding she'd already received from a number of journalists. Thankfully, that had now stopped. The private access to her home had helped, as well as changing all of her numbers and giving herself an anonymous profile on social media.

'My own fault,' she said out loud as she remembered how she'd been castigated for the heartless bitch that she was. The guilt and shame permeated her very soul, and she stood up and walked to the window. It was one of those rare, cloudy days on her part of the island, with no sign of the sun. Looking towards the sea in the distance, the view was still spectacular but this time because the almost black clouds promised a storm was coming. *Just like my life,* Fiona thought.

Knowing her mood was taking her to depths she'd rather not visit, Fiona closed her eyes for a few seconds and took a deep breath. *You can wallow, or you can turn your life around*, she thought, her new mantra for the past few weeks as she'd already decided on the latter.

Their accountant, Mark Fletcher, was visiting within the hour at Fiona's request. She'd seen him a few days after Rob's funeral when he'd said he would look after the business and that she wasn't to worry, and she'd called him a number of times since, but he'd been too busy to see her. Fiona felt her pulse quicken at the thought and her face reddened. She walked to the kitchen to put the kettle on as a distraction to stop herself from becoming annoyed. Determined to embrace her calm, new, self, she made a cup of camomile tea and sat by the window, watching the storm clouds come ever closer.

She hoped he realised she wouldn't be taken for a fool. She'd already told Mr Fletcher that, as the sole beneficiary of Rob's estate, his business empire was now hers. It had been the only comment that had grabbed Mr Fletcher's attention.

'Of course I'll meet with you, as soon as I get a break from running *your* very busy business empire.' Fiona recalled his reply.

She called upstairs. 'Mrs Santos, could you come to the kitchen please?'

She heard the 'Yes, Mrs Fiona,' response as the woman did as requested.

'Would you like a cup of tea?'

'No thank you. Maybe later, after they've left,' Mrs Santos said, as she started taking crockery out of the cupboard. The changes in her employer still amazed her, especially when she decided to be kind, and she didn't want Mrs Green to notice her surprised reaction, in case it upset her.

'I'm expecting Mr Fletcher to be difficult and obstructive,' Fiona said, 'and that's why Mr Brayshaw and his assistant are coming. I'm hoping they'll bamboozle him with legal jargon and make him realise that the only option he has is complete honesty, and that he will, at last, talk me through all Rob's businesses as I requested.'

'I hope so, too, Mrs Fiona.' Her housekeeper told her what she wanted to hear and gave her a weak smile.

No longer obsessed with herself and her own feelings, Fiona noticed that Mrs Santos didn't look happy.

'Is there something wrong, Mrs Santos? You don't look your usual cheery self today.'

Mrs Santos attempted to hide her surprise again while she considered how many times Mrs Green had asked how she was since she'd been working for her and her husband. The answer was twice; once the previous week and now this. It probably wasn't the right time to raise the subject but she decided to anyway. She had a family back home who wouldn't be able to survive without the income from her job, and she didn't know how secure that was. 'I know you've lost so much with Mr Green being…I mean that now Mr Green is in heaven,' she began.

'I doubt very much that my husband is in heaven,' Fiona replied, and there was the former woman her housekeeper knew so well. 'Go on, Mrs Santos, what were you going to say.'

Mrs Santos hesitated.

'It's all right, really.' Fiona smiled in encouragement and the smile looked genuine to Gloria Santos.

'I send most of my money home to my family and if you decide to leave and I no longer have a job–' She put down the cloth she was using to wipe the circular stain from where Fiona's teacup had been sitting next to the kettle, and looked Fiona directly in the eyes. 'Are you going to stay here on the island, and will you want me to keep working for you? Do I need to look for something else? I'm sorry to ask, Mrs Fiona, but…' Mrs Santos

29

stopped talking and looked down. She needed to know but wondered if she'd said too much.

'I don't know my future plans yet, Mrs Santos. But I do know that this villa will always be my home, whether or not I live here permanently. And there will always be a job for you to look after this place for me, again, whether I'm here or not. It's only since Rob died that I've come to value what and also who I have. I'm not sure whether you realise how much I rely on you, Mrs Santos, and I need you as much as you need me.' Fiona turned away from her housekeeper as she felt the tears threaten again. They could sneak up on her unexpectedly and now, minutes before this important meeting, wasn't the time to breakdown. 'Does that help?' she asked, turning back to face her.

'Thank you, Mrs Fiona. Thank you so much. It does help. Yes, it helps a lot. Thank you.'

'That's fine, Mrs Santos. Now, let's get ready for the visitors.'

Mrs Santos carried on with the preparations in the kitchen while Fiona went to the living room and fluffed up a few cushions. The doorbell rang a few minutes later, signalling the arrival of her lawyer and his assistant.

Once they'd settled comfortably and Mrs Santos had brought refreshments, Mr Brayshaw asked for clarification of the situation, prior to the arrival of Mark Fletcher.

'We want to see all of the accounts to include income and expenditure from before Rob died and since. Is that right, Fiona?'

'It is indeed, and I want your accountant to go through them with a fine-tooth comb, and to highlight any discrepancies to me as soon as possible.'

'You mentioned on the phone that something wasn't right? Can you give me more details?'

Fiona looked at Mr Brayshaw and his assistant and hesitated for a moment, trying to find the right words. Trusting your gut instincts was one thing, but trying to explain that to people who dealt in facts and figures was another. 'This will probably sound stupid to you, but…'

While his assistant diplomatically kept his head down, concentrating on whatever was in the documents he held, the lawyer smiled and Fiona realised it was an encouraging, rather than a patronising smile.

'Mrs Green, one of the reasons that I wouldn't represent your husband was because I'd heard rumours that he sailed very close to the wind. Although I didn't attempt to have these rumours substantiated, their source was most reliable and a man that I trust. The rumours about your husband's accountant and right-hand man are even more serious, so please, if you have a gut instinct about some of Mr Fletcher's business practises, please do share the information with me.'

Knowing Rob as she did, Fiona wasn't surprised. 'Thank you, Mr Brayshaw.'

'Not at all. Now what is it that's worrying you?'

Moved by his kindness, Fiona took a tissue out of her pocket and quickly wiped her eyes. She was about to apologise for being so emotional, but decided against it. Getting down to business was the best way to get her emotions in check.

'I've asked Mr Fletcher on a number of occasions to show me the books. At first he said it was too soon after

Rob's death and I wouldn't be able to concentrate to understand them. He told me not to worry saying that he would continue to run the business in the way that Rob wanted, and I'd still get my monthly income. He spoke to me as if I was a child who he was paying an allowance to. I didn't have the energy to argue initially, but now that I've got over the initial shock of Rob's death and started to regain my strength, I want to be involved in the business. When I told Mark that I was going to take over he laughed first of all, as if I were joking. Then he told me that I wasn't capable of doing so. All the while, Clive, he's kept the books from me and I feel he has something to hide.'

'It certainly does sound as if he's hiding something. Or it could be that he wants to continue controlling your vast empire, because that's what it is and it does belong to you. My suggestion is that we get a court order as soon as possible and force him to show us what we're looking for.' Mr Brayshaw looked at his watch. 'He's late.' As he said that, Fiona's phone rang.

'It's him,' she said as she pressed the answer button. '…But we arranged this meeting three weeks ago… I know… but…'

It was a one-sided conversation and by the time Fiona finished the call, Mr Brayshaw already knew that Mark Fletcher wasn't coming.

'He has an emergency regarding my business that he decided not to share with me,' Fiona said. She closed her eyes for a second and clenched her left fist in an attempt not to scream the house down like the former Fiona would have done.

'It's imperative that we get a court order as soon as possible. We need to…'

Mr Brayshaw stopped talking and watched as his client walked to her window and looked out, towards the sea. He knew she was trying to control her emotions rather than admiring the view. His assistant, discreet as ever, concentrated on looking at his notebook as if it contained the secret to eternal life.

A minute passed with nothing but the sounds of Mrs Santos going about her business in the kitchen, and the scratching of the pen on Edward's notebook.

'Can we speak in private?' Fiona asked, turning to face the room.

'Edward is most discreet, Mrs Green, and can be trusted one hundred percent.'

The assistant concentrated on his book but his face reddened.

'No disrespect, Edward,' Fiona said, and the man looked up. 'But would you mind if I had a word with your boss in private.'

Edward looked at Fiona then to his boss. 'Not at all, Mrs Green.' He remained seated until Mr Brayshaw gave a small nod and then he got to his feet.

'If you go to the kitchen, Mrs Santos will make you anything you wish to eat or drink,' Fiona said, closing the door behind him.

'I only smoked for a few years when I was younger and have hardly ever thought about it. But at the moment, I would give anything for a cigarette.' Fiona exhaled deeply and returned to her chair, opposite her lawyer.

He leaned forward. 'You've recently lost your husband in very tragic circumstances. You were involved in a very public love triangle, and you suspect that your husband's right-hand man is involved in illegal business practices and is ripping you off. It's hardly surprising that you need some sort of crutch, Mrs Green. Maybe you should seek the services of a professional to help you to get through these difficult times?'

'Thank you. Perhaps I will. Look, I'd like to wait before getting the court order.' Fiona said. 'I've carried out some research into investigation agencies and intend to engage the services of one to see if I can discover anything about Mark Fletcher, before he tries to hide some of his dealings from me. I have to trust my instincts, as you say, and this is what I want to do before you obtain the court order. Knowing that I'm actually doing something to find out what he's up to will give me back some of the control I feel I've lost in my life, and that'll go a long way to helping me feel better.' She smiled. 'And if we can nail the…'

'Absolutely, Mrs Green,' he replied, with a chuckle.

'I've narrowed it down to two and wondered if you have any experience in this area? If so, perhaps you could help me to choose?'

'It seems that great minds think alike.' He unzipped the leather folder he'd brought with him and handed her a piece of paper. 'This is the company that we use and I recommend them wholeheartedly. But I have to lay my cards on the table. This company is run by my eldest son. We've had excellent results from them and obviously, I trust them completely. But I suppose I must be biased, though I do try not to be.'

Fiona took the paper and read the information then went to the table and picked up her own folder. She handed it to her lawyer. 'These are the two agencies I narrowed it down to.'

Clive recognised the logo straight away and chuckled again. 'It really does look like great minds think alike!'

The three-storey detached building looked like it could have been offices for a swanky law or finance firm, but it was in the wrong part of the city for that. The Satin and Honey club was situated along one of the backstreets in Souva's nightlife district and one would need to know it was there before deciding to visit. The sign on the placard next to the door displayed the words *Private Gentlemen's Club* and the black door gave no clue as to what exactly was on the other side, though most people who'd lived a colourful life could hazard a guess. That's how Mark Fletcher intended to keep it as he sat in his office on the third floor, not even considering what was going on below while he worked on the company accounts. After a little while he sat back and smiled. It had been an exceptionally good month and he'd earned the business much more than Rob Green had prior to his death. The shipping bonuses had helped. So had the money from the new members who were keen to try out the additional services Mark and Suzy had recently added. This had far outweighed losses from those former members who had decided to leave the club. Rob would be turning in his grave if he knew what Mark was doing to his club and his business.

'But you don't do you,' he said out loud, smiling to himself and pressing the buzzer on his desk. 'Suzy, send up one of the new girls, please. I want to test the wares before the customers do.'

Mark left his office and entered the adjoining room. He splashed on some aftershave, changed into his robe, and made sure the champagne was on ice. Then he lay on the king size bed and ran his hand over the leopard patterned bed spread while he awaited the arrival of the girl who he knew would do anything to please him, unlike Grace. Mark smiled to himself. Life wasn't too bad at all.

A while later, Mark had already told the girl to get ready for the night's guests and he headed downstairs to discuss her attributes with Suzy.

'She's pretty special,' he said. 'I want you to start her at level two, but keep an eye on her. If she's as diplomatic as she is talented, we can move her to the top level pretty quickly and she's going to be one of our stars. Where did you find her?'

Suzy smiled. 'I've been putting feelers out and it seems to have worked. She didn't want to be a domestic and said she was willing to do anything to earn good money.'

'Okay. Well pay her a decent salary and keep her with the others who know nothing. I'm sure the clients will love her and we should get a good number of months out of her before I decide her long-term future. Are we all ready for the minister?'

'Yes. His favourites are ready and waiting. They took some convincing after what happened to…'

'Never mind that. I've had a word and he's assured me it won't happen again.'

'All the same, Mark, I've had to give them a little something to calm their nerves, and they're still asking after their friend.'

'What did you tell them?'

'That her mother was very ill and we released her from her contract so she could go home. They're not stupid and they know what the minister's like. I'm not sure whether they believed me.'

'It doesn't really matter. They've all willingly signed our contract and must have seen some of the others come and go. Keep telling them that we only want girls here who want to work for us and that we've released some from their contracts early. The troublemakers have gone now and I don't think we'll see any more for a while – it's good money and that's what most are after – but keep your eyes and ears open just in case.'

Suzy kept nodding as Mark talked. But he noticed she stopped herself from biting her lip occasionally while she listened and she went to say something, but hesitated. He knew her motivation was the same as his and wasn't everyone the same? He decided not to make her ask.

'We make a good team,' Mark said, and Suzy knew that was the most praise she was likely to get from her boss. 'And I have something for you, as promised.' He put a hand in his inside jacket pocket and took out a wad of money, rolled together with an elastic band.

'Thank you, Mr Fletcher,' she said. 'I enjoy working for you.' She took the money. 'I'll get everyone ready for the night shift.' Suzy made a fist around the money and left the room. For the second time that day Mark smiled to himself, smug about the way his life had taken a turn for the better since he'd taken full control of the business after Rob's death. His plan to buy Fiona out was also coming along nicely and Mark decided to visit her the following week, to put the proposals to her.

Chapter 4

The night was black and silent with only a quarter moon lighting up the sky as Wee Jimmy's henchman, Janus, parked the car and gave him a torch. They made their way to the cave for Jimmy to inspect the goods before the boat sailed for Italy. The girls formed a trail from the cave to the sea and were herded onto the boat by three of the five men who would form the crew and the guards for the journey.

'Are we one short?' Jimmy asked, and one of the men nodded towards the cave.

'Bit of trouble, boss,' he said.

Jimmy and Janus rushed to the cave where a woman was sitting with her arms hugging her knees, refusing to move. One of the men spoke to her in English, their common language.

'If you don't walk, I'll drag yer.'

'Do it,' she replied, defiant despite the fear in her eyes.

'Want to end up the same way as the last one who wouldn't play ball?'

'Shut up!' Wee Jimmy told him. 'The less she knows, the better.' He looked at the girl that he'd had a part in hand picking. She was trouble, but well worth it for the price she attracted, and that particular buyer would always pay more for those he had to tame. *And what became of the girls after he'd tamed them?* Jimmy wondered briefly, before smiling to himself. One of his employees gave him a strange look which Jimmy noticed, and the smile disappeared off Jimmy's face as he stared him down and the man looked away. He didn't give a damn what happened to the women as long as they got there alive and in a good enough shape for the buyers to pay the agreed prices. This was business and he couldn't let the crew or the girls think he would allow this type of behaviour. He could see the defiance in her eyes as she looked up at him and the other men were waiting for him to tell them what to do. None of them saw it coming as he moved quickly and in two movements he knelt on the sandy floor and then raised his hand and slapped her. The force of the slap threw her head back against the rock. Angelica shouted in pain and the sound echoed throughout the cave. She put her hand to the back of her head and felt blood.

'Do you want some more of that?' Jimmy asked.

Angelica knew she was beaten. 'No, no.' She pulled herself to her feet, cowering away from him, and then clutched at her stomach. 'I have to pee,' she said, and hurried behind an enormous rock before they could stop her. She squatted and peed as quickly as she could and then took off both jackets. Angelica wiped the blood from her hand onto the small, pink, denim jacket which she'd been wearing under the heavier jacket, and put on the heavier jacket hoping it would keep her warm on the journey to wherever they were taking her. She put the pink jacket on the ground and put two heavy stones on it so it wouldn't be washed out to sea by the tide. She prayed silently that the men wouldn't go behind the rocks before they left the cave, and that somebody would eventually find it.

It was her last act of defiance; she knew they were thought of as third-class citizens, or even less than farm animals, and didn't expect anyone to do anything about the way they were treated, but if she believed that somebody, somewhere cared, then it was a small glimmer of hope in a sea of despair and uncertainty. She needed that to hold on to in the difficult times ahead. She wished with all her heart that she'd stayed as a domestic and hadn't wanted more out of life. After murmuring one last quick, silent prayer, she hurried back to where the men were standing. Her cheek still stung where Jimmy had hit her, and her head was sore but she knew there was nothing she could do. Her heart beating like it would jump out of her chest, and eyes flitting from side to side, she was led towards the boat. With one man on either side of her, Angelica knew there was no way she could escape. She was hurried towards the sea and to a future life of God only knew what—but Angelica suspected it would include all types of physical assault, abject misery, and loss of freedom.

There was only one thing of which she was most certain: whatever they had in store for her, she had absolutely no say in the matter.

Elena saw an image of a delicate looking hand with bright red nail varnish on the fingernails. She woke with a start when the index finger beckoned her. Realising it was a dream, she took a moment to compose herself and return to the real world of wakefulness. She felt Matt's body moving next to hers and she turned to look at him.

He was walking through the train carriages. Bodies were strewn in his way and the carriage was on its side, but still he continued to walk. When he got to the far end of the carriage, he was transported to the start and was back walking along the carriage, over and over again. Amongst all the mess and mayhem was a man dressed in a suit. He was reading the Financial Times and barely looked up as he nodded every time Matt passed. Matt was drawn to what was left of the Filipino girl who had been sitting

opposite him. She was wearing bright red nail varnish and
sometimes he could see her, other times she was in a blue plastic bag.

'I'm going to help you,' he told her. 'We'll catch the person
who did this to you.'

When Elena heard his undecipherable mutterings
and saw that his shaking was becoming worse, she knew
it was time to wake him. She put a gentle hand on his
arm.

'Matt, Matt. It's all right, Matt. Wake up, it's a bad
dream.'

His eyes opened and Elena saw the panic in them
when, at first, he had no idea where he was. Then he
remembered and closed his eyes again for a few seconds.
The next time when he opened them, Elena was relieved
to see that *her* Matt was back.

'I'm sorry, did I wake you?'

'Not at all. A bad dream woke me too, then I
noticed your discomfort. I thought it best to wake you.'

'Thanks, love,' he said, then sat up in bed. 'What
time is it?'

'Five o'clock. Are you all right?'

'I'm fine now that I'm awake. You go back to sleep.
I'm going to get a coffee and I'll take Jenny out as soon
as it gets lighter.'

Jenny stepped out of her bed, stretched her back
legs and yawned. Then she ambled over to Matt's side of
the bed and they said good morning to each other. She
walked round to Elena's side of the bed and Elena petted
Jenny in greeting.

'What a lovely way to start the day,' Elena said.

'She's been a great help since the train crash,' Matt
said, and it seemed to Elena that he might be ready to tell
her more.

41

'I'm glad she's given you comfort, Matt. I hope I can help too, whatever you want me to do.'

'You already do help, Elena.'

'That's what I want to hear. I'll get the coffee on and come out with you and Jenny. We can have a Nanna nap this afternoon if we're tired,' Elena replied, heading for the bathroom.

An hour later they were on their way to the dog-friendly Griffon's Point Beach. Unspoilt by the tourist trade, the beach was the other side of Griffon's Rest and was accessible from both ends. They parked in a cleared area that was used as a car park, but theirs was the only vehicle there. The sun was rising and there were few clouds in the sky, giving the promise of a lovely day. As yet, the morning sun hadn't warmed the air, sand, or sea. The dew on the grass verge shone like crystals as the sun cast its rays on the individual blades.

Elena was dressed in her three-quarter length sports trousers and a t-shirt, but wore a fleece to combat the bite of winter. Not yet acclimatised, Matt wore shorts and a t-shirt with a light fleece. They headed down the slope towards the beach.

'It's going to be a beautiful day,' he said. 'People at home would die for this weather in the summer, never mind the winter. We're very lucky.'

'Lucky for where we were born and that we met each other, Matt, and I'll be forever grateful for that. But luck has nothing to do with the rest of it.' She gestured around her with an arm. 'I've worked hard to achieve this lifestyle and I know you have too. And we'll be even more fortunate if we can do something to rid you of your demons.'

They stopped walking. Matt took Elena's hand and squeezed it. As they watched Jenny running along the beach and chasing the waves, Matt sensed that the time was right. He spoke quietly as they began walking again, this time, hand in hand. 'It's not pleasant seeing dead bodies at any time, but the best I can say is that I got used to it in the force. The way I dealt with murders and the scumbags who commit the crimes was to put up a sort of emotional defensive shield and it became part of the job. It was always a good feeling when you could tell the victim's loved ones that the person who had committed the crime had been caught. Don't get me wrong, Elena, nothing can make up for the loss of a loved one, but it does help if they feel that justice has been done and they can then start to move on with their lives.'

Elena smiled encouragement and Matt continued. 'My shield must have been down the day of the train crash. A car was out of control and sped onto the railway track. The train driver had no chance and the carriage flipped after the impact. God it was awful!'

'I can't even begin to imagine,' she said. 'How bad were your injuries?'

'A broken arm and leg, cuts, bruises and mild concussion, and I was one of the lucky ones. I didn't realise at the time that getting over my physical injuries would be a doddle, compared to what was going on in my head. When I was in hospital, the painkillers more or less knocked me out. Eight people died but it could have been a lot worse. The nightmares started as soon as I got home and it was always that girl in the same carriage as me. Her mangled body and–' Matt stopped both talking and walking and Elena put her arms around him. They hugged for a few moments until Jenny came sprinting back and tried to squeeze herself in between them. Matt found strength from Elena's embrace and, after he patted Jenny and reassured her that all was well, they watched her sprint back to the sea while they continued walking.

'I felt ashamed about the way it affected me and when I was first off sick and just speaking to family and friends by phone, thought I'd hidden it pretty well. I don't know how, but Kayleigh realised something was wrong after we'd spoken one day. She called Keith and he came around. I pretended to be out but he was persistent, and when I let him in, he was shocked at the way I'd let myself go and the mess in the house. Keith wanted to stay for a while but I wouldn't let him, so he checked on me every day and reported back to Kayleigh. At the time they drove me nuts, but looking back I realise they saved me. Without them I might have ended it all.'

'Oh, Matt, you poor thing. How awful.' Elena's words sounded like platitudes to her ears but from his look she could tell he knew they were from the heart.

'It's been a fight ever since, Elena, but better since I decided to see the police psychiatrist though it did take me a while to open up to her. She gave me coping mechanisms and I'm a lot better now. Being able to concentrate on Jenny and having the support of my daughter and Keith in the early days after the accident was a life-saver, literally.'

'Does your son know?'

'I didn't want to worry Glenn so asked Kayleigh not to mention it. Perhaps I'll tell him one day, but not for now. The nightmares were coming less often but seeing the woman in the bondu was a shock. It might be hard to believe, Elena, but the girl on the train and the one in the bondu could be sisters. I saw her face after you left and they look so much alike. I couldn't do anything to help the family of the girl on the train and I think that was one of the reasons it's stayed with me for so long, as well as being quite a traumatic event of course. But if there's anything I can do to get justice for that girl on the bondu, I will. For her, her loved ones, and for my own peace of mind.'

'How are you going to do that, Matt?'

'I've agreed to help George with some routine detective work when you go back to work. He's looking for a connection with other crimes from an operation they're working on. Keeping busy will help to keep any dark thoughts at bay, while I'm awake, anyway. I'm broken goods, Elena, and will understand if this is all too much for you to cope with. I should have told you before. You're the only one who knows exactly how I feel, though the psychiatrist could probably guess.'

'I'm in this for the long haul, Matt. I haven't been this happy in years and there's no way I'm going to let what happened to you split us up, broken goods or not.'

'Well prepare for some sleepless nights then!'

They both laughed and then Matt continued, 'I found it difficult to concentrate when I returned to work and was eventually medically discharged. My boss, Dale, knew I had PTSD, but didn't know the extent of the problem. Since then I've been working on getting better and the nightmares have been coming less and less. But certain events trigger my sub-conscious and, like I said, that girl was–'

Elena waited but Matt was deep in thought. She decided it was time to change the subject and let go of his hand, reaching down to take off her trainers and socks. 'Shall we go for a paddle?'

'I thought you said it was too cold.' Matt said, grinning at her, his mood lifting.

'It is. Come on, I'll race you,' she said, and was off and running. By the time Matt had taken off his trainers, she was already dipping her toes in the sea and squealing.

Matt waded right in up to his knees. 'You're not wrong, this is bloody freezing!' Happy to see her humans enjoying themselves, Jenny bounded over incoming waves until she was out of her depth and then swam back to the shore where Elena was still deciding whether she was going in further. She shook herself and half soaked Elena.

'Arrgh,' she shouted, and headed towards Matt.

It had the effect that Elena had hoped for and the worry lines had disappeared from Matt's face by the time they decided enough was enough, and it was time to get out.

'I'm glad I brought towels with us,' Elena said, when they returned to the car.

Matt nodded as he towelled the dog dry and then concentrated on himself. 'Thanks, love,' he said, without looking at her, and Elena knew he wasn't only thanking her for the towels.

Chapter 5

Jezz Brayshaw had happily agreed to take on the investigation on behalf of Fiona Green. The pay was good and the case was interesting, to say the least. Fiona had pushed Mark Fletcher, the family accountant for further information, which he had agreed to, albeit reluctantly, and had left some paperwork for her to look through. Fiona photocopied the information and handed the books back to Mark and when Jezz looked at the information, he quickly discovered that it had been recorded in such a way that the average layman would be confused—as a trained accountant, he hadn't found it easy:

Green Enterprises as the company was called, was primarily a money-lending business, but by delving deep into the books, Jezz discovered that a number of entries involving payments to a new company had been added after the date of Mr Green's death. This company was entitled *JW Holdings* and, having Googled the hell out of the name, Jezz had come up with nothing. There were also a number of other payments to various companies and when Jezz dug deeper, he discovered that the latter payments all ended up in the same bank account – one of those belonging to Mark Fletcher. It could be that Mr Fletcher had carried out extra work and had earned bonuses, but if that were the case, why hadn't he been honest and shown the payments made to him in the same way that his monthly wages and some expenses were shown on the spreadsheets and in the books? The whole thing stank of dishonesty and Jezz sat back to think for a moment. Then he picked up the phone and called his father's office. The PA put him through straight away.

'Hello, Jeremy. Have you found anything?' His father was one of only two people who called him by his full name (his late mother being the other) and it always threw Jezz. He dispensed with any niceties and got straight down to business.

'The man must know Mrs Green would have no idea what she was looking for, and by the look of the books, he's either too cocky to believe she would hire anyone else to investigate, or too lazy or useless to do a proper job of hiding the entries. I think he's bent, Dad, and using her lack of knowledge to screw her for every penny he can get out of her. But there's more to it. Something dodgy's going on but I don't know exactly what yet.'

'Have you any proof, son?'

'No. It's gut instinct at the moment, but that's based on some of the entries since Mr Green's death. A company called *JW Holdings,* to be precise. Nothing paid to them until a few weeks after Mr Green died and multiple payments since then.'

'*JW Holdings?* For some reason that name rings a bell. Let me have a think about it and I'll get back to you if I remember anything.'

'Okay. And I'll carry on with my investigation. But I need to inform Mrs Green so that she can freeze her assets and stop Mark Fletcher from filtering funds from the company.'

'If you do that now we may never know who this other company is and Mark Fletcher will be free to go and screw someone else. Let's see what the rest of your investigation comes up with. I'll have a quiet word with Fiona Green and advise her of our course of action.'

'Really, Dad?'

'Yes, Jeremy, really. It'll give me an excuse to call on her. Keep me informed.' His father ended the call before Jezz had a chance to ask any questions totally unrelated to money. It was the first time since his mother had died almost seven years before that his father had mentioned he wanted to talk to another woman, and this gave Jezz more to think about than investigating Mrs Green's books.

A few days later, all paths that Jezz had followed in obtaining more information about JW Holdings had come up blank. He knew the only way to possibly discover further information was by surveillance. About to ring his father to discuss possible options, his phone rang first.

'Hello, Dad,'

'I need to meet you as soon as possible. In private.'

Knowing he must have information that his father didn't want to discuss over the phone, Jezz suggested a stroll along the quieter part of a promenade alongside one of the capital's beach fronts.

Later that day, the pair walked along a path which was packed with tourists during the summer but was fairly quiet during winter. The only others were locals, most of them out on their fitness regimes. As the sun hung in the sky over the Mediterranean, its rays sparkled in the sea and the warm glow meant it was pleasant enough to walk without the need for jackets. They caught up on trivia until they had walked far enough where there were only a few locals about, and then headed in the direction of the five-star hotels.

Clive waited until two women jogging behind them had passed and then got straight to the point. 'A man known as Wee Jimmy Wilson is the owner of JW

Holdings. Edward's photographic memory is amazing and as soon as I mentioned it to him, he reminded me of a potential client who'd emailed a while ago, asking us to represent him.'

'You've dealt with the company then?'

'Not at all, Jeremy. The only thing that Edward could find out about them was from an old newspaper archive in the UK saying that the company had gone into liquidation. He couldn't find anything else and after a bit of digging, neither could I. I had a bad feeling about the potential client, too, so turned him down and I think he's since returned to the UK. I have my reputation to think of and if my gut instinct tells me something's a bit off, I can be choosy about who I represent.'

'But what if you're wrong, Dad?'

Clive laughed. 'It doesn't matter. If I don't take them on, then I'll never know. Business is good, Jeremy, and I can choose to be picky. And if I do discover I've made a mistake later down the line? So what? Nobody's perfect.'

'Fair enough. So this Wee Jimmy Wilson, I presume he's Scottish with a name like that?'

'I think that's a fair assumption, but I have no idea. I've had Edward do some research but interestingly, when Edward looked again, even that newspaper information he discovered a while ago has now disappeared, and we've come up blank. Whatever Mr Wilson does, he's not public with it and I can only presume that his dealings are all carried out on the dark web,' Clive said, and was met with silence. He gave it a few seconds. 'Well, son?'

Jezz stopped walking and looked out to sea, and his father did the same. The wind, usually present on winter

50

afternoons, hadn't arrived and the sea was calm and peaceful. Jezz felt the stillness wash over him and, having now made his decision, started walking again.

'This is new territory for me, Dad. I've dealt with cheating husbands and wives, fraudsters, all sorts of liars and other petty criminals, but nothing sinister enough to take me onto the dark web or to investigate the type of people who use it. I'm not sure I–'

'We know that Mr Fletcher is ripping off Mrs Green, so that's enough for him to be charged if we take this further,' his father interrupted. 'But there's a lot more to it than that. I think it's time to tell both Mrs Green of our suspicions and the police. But let me speak to my contact in the Souva Police and get his advice before we speak to Fiona. I don't want her to be collateral damage or to be worried about something that she's had no control over.'

'But she owns the business.'

'Only on paper, Jeremy. She has no idea what's happening on a day-to-day basis, and I think that Mr Fletcher has taken advantage of the situation. A grieving widow, untrained in her late husband's dealings, is a prime candidate for him to do whatever he wants and to get away with it too.'

'Fair point.'

'And I'm determined that she doesn't get into any trouble because of him. I'll call you as soon as I've spoken to the police and we can meet up again. Now, do you fancy a coffee and you can tell me all about how it's going with Carly.'

Now it was Jezz's turn to laugh. 'Yes to coffee, but no to Carly. She's so last month, Dad,' he said, deciding not to tell his father that Carly was still bothering him.

'Another one? If your mother were with us she'd be asking if you're ever going to settle down.'

'Carly would have loved that, but it wasn't meant to be. Anyway, I think Mum would tell me that life is short and to go and enjoy myself.'

Clive squeezed his son's arm and they gave each other a sad smile. 'Perhaps you're right, son. Let's go and get that coffee.'

The next four days were like a mini holiday for Matt and Elena as they visited a number of tourist attractions on the island: the more popular beaches; the ancient ruins; the towns with shops that sold tacky tourist items as well as jewellery shops with items made from Souvia Stone, the island's semi-precious mottled stone of cream and green, the shade varying depending on where it had been mined. They also visited museums, along with other historical sites. Matt already felt at home but did so even more when the truck arrived with his belongings, including the therapeutic bed that he'd bought shortly after the crash that had helped to ease his aching joints.

'I'm not sure I even need this now,' he said, 'but it's so comfortable.'

'We'll give it a shot,' Elena said. 'Look at Jenny, now that is one happy bunny.'

The dog's bed had arrived and she was lying in it, her two front paws around Foxy, her favourite cuddly toy. It looked like Jenny was cuddling her toy and she was snoring gently.

'That makes two of us, Elena,' Matt said, before kissing her.

One of the removal men rolled his eyes at his mate before they carried the bed upstairs.

They spent the day and the night unpacking and sorting out what was to go where. After a tiring day, both slept a dreamless sleep.

'I have news for you, Matt. Our new cleaner is starting today,' Elena said, a few days before returning to work.

'I didn't know we were getting a cleaner?'

'I'm sure I mentioned it to you. Anyway, I know you're not a fan of housework and I don't want to spend all my down time cleaning. And this one sheds like it's going out of fashion,' she added, giving Jenny a big cuddle as she did so. 'Analyn works part-time at the hotel. She's looking for full-time work so I thought she could come to us twice a week. She's fab, Matt. Really efficient, trustworthy and friendly. One of the few staff I've never had any issues with.'

'How come she wants to change her hours?'

'She was working part-time for two other families, but one has recently returned to France and Analyn has a son who's about to start Uni back home in the Philippines. She sends money home to support her family and needs to work full-time to do so. I already sponsor her for the work in the hotel, so it makes sense for her to work here, especially as we want a cleaner.'

'Oh, we do, do we?'

'Yes, Matt, of course we do. Unless you want to do all the housework…? No, I thought not. The other family she works for doesn't treat her very well, and apparently that's not unusual. I'm looking at giving her more hours in the hotel, too. One of my younger staff is leaving to go and study in the U.K., so Analyn will fill that post, but not until after Easter. She'll be able to leave the family she works for and will be full-time with me.'

53

'It's a shame that she has to work for a family who treat her badly in order to send money home to her family. What an awful situation,' Matt said. 'But at least she'll be able to see some light at the end of the tunnel with your help, and Easter's not too far away.'

Elena had asked Analyn to arrive at 9 o'clock on her first day, after they'd finished their breakfast. Jenny barked a few seconds before the bell rang and Elena answered the door. Matt heard them chatting before they came into the kitchen.

'Hello, sir,' the woman greeted him. 'I'm Analyn. Nice to meet you.'

'You too, Analyn,' Matt said, holding his hand out in greeting. 'And please call me Matt.'

'Yes, sir,' she replied, and they all laughed.

'I'll show you around,' Elena said, and Matt heard the women talking as he went back to reading his book.

When Elena returned to the kitchen she was alone and they could hear Analyn moving around upstairs.

'Analyn said another woman has gone missing.'

'What do you mean, another woman?'

'Another one. She's the second recently, if you count the poor girl we found in the bondu. The Filipino workers are so far away from their families that they rely on each other a lot and have their own communities outside their workplaces. They meet every Sunday on their day off to catch up and news travels like wildfire. Last Sunday, one of Analyn's friends told her that her niece had gone missing. She said she's ambitious, had no intention of doing domestic work, and would do what it took to earn good money. They think she went to work in a club but aren't sure. Anyway, she works nights and

54

usually returns to her lodgings around six o'clock in the morning, but she didn't last Saturday.'

'Have they reported it?'

'Yup, of course, and I expect she'll go on the list along with all of the other people who go missing. Some want to be found and others don't and I have no idea which category this girl falls into. But I think it's suspicious, especially since we found that poor–'

They heard Analyn coming down the stairs and Elena stopped talking as she walked into the room.

'I'm sorry to hear about your friend's daughter, Analyn. I hope they find her safe and well,' Matt said.

'Me too, Matt Sir,' Analyn said. 'My friend Gloria is very upset. I'm going to help her look for Rosalee when I'm not working. We have to find her.'

'We hope you do,' Elena said.

Analyn gave a weak smile and then asked Elena to show her to the cleaning products which she took out of the cupboard and separated into two groups. 'These are good, but not these,' she said, all business now. 'Can I give you a list to buy what I need?'

'Of course. I'll get them tomorrow when Elena's back in work.'

Satisfied, Analyn took what she needed and made her way back up the stairs.

Chapter 6

'Clive?' George said when he answered the call. 'I haven't heard from you in ages. How are things?'

'Life's good thanks, George. Any chance you can spare me some time? I have some information you need to know about.

Later that day, the two men met. Clive passed copies of the transactions he'd discovered to George, who promised to have them looked at and to get back to his friend.

'Do you know how long it will take?'

'I've no idea, but now you've reported this to me, I need you to keep Mrs Green out of the loop for now. If Jezz has got this right, you might just have saved the widow's skin.'

George returned to the station and passed the information onto the Fraud and Financial Crimes Investigation Department.

His boss called him in the following day. 'We think Wee Jimmy Wilson is active again in Souvia.'

George raised an eyebrow. 'We had no record of his return to the island so he must have come in illegally, by boat. No idea when. But as far as the *whys* are concerned, we know he's a good-for-nothing and is here because he can't compete with the big-time gangsters in the U.K. How do you want to proceed?'

'We have no idea where he is, but the man likes to strut his stuff, so shouldn't be too difficult to find. I've received the go-ahead this morning to bug Mark Fletcher's apartment in Souva and if you put a team onto him, we should be able to track down Wee Jimmy that way. Tell Clive Brayshaw that we're dealing with it. They will need to stall the widow. Try to make sure she doesn't become impatient and confront Mark Fletcher. That would ruin the investigation and stop us from discovering what they're up to. I've got a feeling we might be onto something big here, George.'

'I think you're right, boss.' George left the office and got down to work straight away.

'It's me,' the voice on the phone said to Wee Jimmy. Neither number displayed on the burner phones. 'I have someone who's outgrown her usefulness here and I want her on the next boat. Is there room?'

'I'll make sure there is. Shall I collect from the usual place?'

'Yes.' Mark got up from his office and headed to the bathroom. He closed the door behind him, unzipped his trousers and sat on the toilet. 'Be there at quarter to midnight. I'll get Suzy to give her a little something so she won't wake up until tomorrow, all nice and fresh for her journey.'

'Got it. See you later.' Jimmy hung up and took a hammer out of his desk drawer. He dropped the phone to the floor and smashed it. Then he walked to the wall, lifted off a picture and put it on the floor displaying a safe with a circular combination lock. He keyed in the correct number. A satisfying click followed and the door swung open.

He lifted out a phone from the stack inside, picked up a new sim card, and one of the many wads of notes. His fingers hovered over the pistol and he picked it up. If he needed a gun to deal with a sleeping woman, he'd definitely lost the plot, but he might need it for the later operation so planned to take it with him. Always best to be prepared, just in case. He put the money in his pocket and put everything else down while he locked the safe and returned the picture to the wall.

Jimmy took Janus with him to be his bitch, as he liked to call his henchmen. Winter was the quietest time for the island but there were still enough cars on the streets for them not to raise suspicion and Janus drove so as not to draw any attention. They went to the edge of what was the main tourist area in the city and on into the backstreets of the nightlife district, heading to the three storey buildings where the club was situated. Janus carried on past the street the club was on and took a left, two streets behind it, heading for the two houses where the women were accommodated. He took another left and turned into the gulley behind the houses–it was more than large enough for the car to drive through.

The headlights caught something scurrying out of the rubbish, startled by the car's stark headlights. The streetlights at the end of the gulley weren't powerful enough to shine any light and Jimmy took a few seconds for his eyes to adjust to the dark. Once they did, he made a visual check of the other houses in the area. If any lights were on in other properties, the curtains or blinds were thick enough to shroud them in darkness. In contrast, as they opened the back gate to the property they were visiting, the lights from the kitchen lit up the outside area. Two men were sitting at a wooden table on the patio outside the door smoking cigarettes and ignoring each other as they played with their smart phones. As soon as they heard the gate, they were up on their feet, ready for action. As he approached, Jimmy noticed any tension disappear from the men as they recognised him and Janus.

'Boss said go straight up,' one of the men, Frank, said. 'She's in the third room on the left.'

'Is the boss here?'

'No, he's at the club. Suzy's with her.'

Jimmy's eye twitched and he tried to hide his annoyance. 'We'll wait until the boss comes back. I need to speak to him.'

'He's not coming back tonight, Wee Jimmy. Just get on with it.'

Jimmy raised a fist and the security man who'd remained quiet until then stepped in front of his mate.

'Frank's just passing on the message. They were Mr Fletcher's words, not his. I'll take you up, if you're ready to collect the girl?'

Placated, Wee Jimmy gave Frank a warning look. Satisfied when the man's eyes dropped to the ground he turned to the other. 'Lead the way.'

The guard did as requested and less than ten minutes later, Jimmy and Janus walked out of the kitchen door, Janus carrying a heavily drugged woman wrapped in a blanket.

The two guards waited until they heard the car engine start up.

'He's a muppet,' Frank said.

'He is, but the boss likes him. Try not to wind him up next time, eh?'

Frank laughed and they lit up fresh cigarettes and got back to playing with their phones.

When Mark Fletcher was heard speaking about a club, an undercover team was put onto it. The operation was set up and the undercover team waited in the apartment they had rented right opposite the house where the club was located. It was the early hours of the morning and the streetlamps cast a yellow glow on the pavements. The men in the apartment watched as a man in a business suit approached the door. His head was down and he was wearing a hat and clearly, did not want to be recognised.

A radio buzzed into action. 'That's the Education Minister approaching the door,' the undercover cop said, 'and they've let him in.'

Less than a minute later, another man approached. 'Here's our man,' the undercover cop informed the team and they watched as the policeman, posing as a visiting businessman after a bit of action, was admitted. Mark Fletcher followed shortly after.

They listened as Brian, known for this operation as James Henderson of Henderson Recycling Ltd, was asked about his preferences. There were no questions about how he'd found the club – that had been established in his cover story before entry. George had taken a chance and they'd been told the undercover was an associate of the Education Minister. Knowing the minister's reputation for his bad temper and for sacking employees that crossed him, George took a gamble that the minister would not be questioned about his so-called business associate. If he was, it was likely he would either reprimand the man who dared to question him, or he would admit to knowing such a rich man with a carefully built reputation. By the time the operation was over it wouldn't matter.

James Henderson left the building less than an hour later, having successfully placed bugs in three rooms and the entrance area.

The day before Valentine's Day was when the team got their lucky break. Mark Fletcher made a call about a shipment. It was via one of his burner phones and they only heard his half of the conversation, but that, together with the rest of the intelligence gathered, was enough to know that a ship was to leave the following night and would most likely contain human cargo.

Chapter 7

It was Elena's final day off.

'Shall we have an easy day today?' Matt asked over a breakfast of poached eggs on toast with avocado, one of Elena's favourites. 'Maybe a leisurely walk along Griffon's Point Beach, followed by lunch out and a movie night tonight?'

'Sounds like a plan,' Elena said, taking the mickey out of Matt's favourite saying and he nudged her. 'Except for the movie night. I'm going to have an early night as it'll probably be chaos at work like it usually is after I've had some time off.'

It was a sunny day, though there was a chill in the air and it was windy on the beach. They decided to walk the full-length and back this time, and not to follow Jenny into the sea. As they headed towards the far end, Matt noticed what looked like caves in the distance. The tide was out and Jenny came out of the sea, heading towards them, eager to explore.

As they neared the end, Matt looked up to the cliffs high above them. 'We'll have to drive up there one day, Elena, and take a look around. It looks desolate but I bet the view is stunning.'

'It is, Matt, and we don't have to drive. If we go around the bay here…' she pointed, '…we can walk for a bit and then look at the caves. There's a narrow path all the way up, too. It's a bit steep but we can still walk it.' They carried on walking and as they approached, Matt was astounded to see entrances to two caves. 'How come I didn't know about these?' he asked.

Elena laughed. 'Well, for one, we haven't walked this far before, and two, you only see the entrances when the tide is out. Unless you know they're there, you just assume that they're part of the rock face. Rumour has it this used to be a smuggler's beach you know, back in the day. And that the smugglers used the caves to hide stuff.'

'That sounds interesting. When did it stop? Tell me more.'

'That's all I know, Matt. I'm generally too busy at work to stand and listen to gossip and old folklore.'

'Well, that's me told!'

She laughed. 'I'll buy you a book about it, and then you can decide what's fact and what's the usual nonsense. Come on. If we hurry, we can have a quick look inside one of the caves if you don't mind getting a bit wet.'

Matt was too curious to worry about getting wet and he crouched down to follow her into the cave. 'Wow,' he said, looking around. 'I didn't expect this.'

The small entrance opened into a bigger area which was tall enough for them both to stand upright. It smelled of sea salt and something else that Matt couldn't identify straight away. *Jenny can smell it too,* Matt thought as the dog ran around ahead of them, sniffing the air as she did so and exploring the nooks and crannies that would have been difficult for Matt and Elena to reach.

'What is that?' Elena asked.

Matt shrugged his shoulders.

Elena walked towards the back of the small cave. 'If I didn't know better, I'd say that smells like some sort of perfume.'

Matt had a think but before replying. Jenny came trotting towards him carrying what looked like an item of clothing.

'What have you got there, girl?' he asked, surprised that the item hadn't been washed out to sea when the tide came in.

'Look, something's dropped from it.' Elena pointed to the wet sandy floor and headed towards whatever had dropped off or out of a pocket of what Jenny was carrying, while Matt inspected the item.

'It's a pink denim jacket,' he called to Elena. 'And it stinks of perfume and cigar smoke and there's a… Oh heck.'

'What is it, Matt?' Elena asked as she walked back to him. Without giving him a chance to answer, she continued, 'I've found this, card, it says honey or something honey, hang on…' The card was damp and floppy and she wiped some of the dirt and sand off it. 'I'll have to get back out into the light to read this.'

'There's a stain on this jacket, Elena, and I think it's dried blood.'

'What the hell? What is it with you that we can't go for a walk without finding something a bit iffy?'

Matt laughed. 'You mean us, Elena, and it's probably nothing. Somebody maybe fell on one of the rocks and broke their skin or something.' He didn't believe a word of it and neither did she.

Outside the cave, the pink writing on the damp black card was clearer. Elena held it up to the light. 'It says, *Satin and Honey Gentlemen's Club*, but look at it, Matt.' She handed him the card which had an outline of a semi-naked young woman, partly covered by a wisp of satin and the words in the middle.

'Looks more like a knocking shop to me. Let's pass this information to George or Chloe and see what they make of it.'

Elena agreed, and took her phone out of her pocket. There was no signal and they had to walk quite a way down the beach before she could make the call. 'George is out,' she said. 'But Chloe's going to stop by my office tomorrow and she's asked me to put them in a bag until then.'

'Okay. Shall we just go home? I've lost my appetite.'

They were unlocking the front door when Matt's phone rang to indicate an incoming video call. 'It's Keith,' he said.

'I thought he'd agreed not to bother you until I was back at work,' Elena said.

Matt gave her an apologetic look and answered the call, heading for the study.

'I'm sorry to bother you, mate, but thought you'd like to know. A boat capsized in the Mediterranean last night and a number of people died.'

'Oh no. Refugees?'

'That's the thing, Matt, they weren't refugees. According to one of the survivors they were forced to get onto the boat at gunpoint and their kidnappers threatened to harm their families if they disobeyed. They were being taken to mainland Europe. This is people-trafficking, Matt, or modern-day slavery to be precise.'

Matt was listening quietly, his mind already working overtime. The signal was weak and started buffering and he waited for the video to reconnect.

'Are you there, Matt?'

'I am, yes. Go on.'

'The boat came from Souvia, Matt.'

'Do you know if any of the survivors are Filipino?'

'I don't. But I do know that the passengers are attractive women in their late teens or early twenties and it doesn't take a rocket scientist to work out what they're being sold into.'

'Twenty-first century slavery,' said Matt, 'and these poor women are enticed into what they think is going to be a life of glamour, then forced to work as sex slaves. Any survivors?

'Ten so far.'

'The girls, crew or runners?'

'Confirmed reports say that nine of the girls have definitely survived. There may be more. As for the crew and runners, they are one and the same. They have one in custody and we don't yet know whether the others have drowned or have been rescued. But you know how it is. The people who run these trips will be small players in a big game and will only be told what they need to know.'

'Where was the boat heading and what happened?'

'Towards Italy when it capsized. It was supposed to hold a maximum of twenty passengers but the early reports indicate that it was jam-packed. The authorities are not sure how many yet because they don't know if all the bodies have been recovered, but they estimate that over forty people were on the boat. Do you think this is all connected with the missing women?'

'I've had quite an eventful first week in Souvia, Keith,' Matt answered, explaining about the young girl they'd found on the bondu and the discovery in the cave that morning. 'These have to be connected, don't they?'

'I agree.'

'I need you to find out as much information as you can, Keith, so we can discover who tried to murder the girl we found on the bondu and get justice for her and her family, and for those of the other victims.'

'Okay. Has she woken up yet?'

'No, she's still in a deep coma and apparently it's too early to say whether she will ever wake up.'

'I see. Are you working with the local police on this case?'

Matt hesitated before answering. 'Yes.'

'Matt?'

'There's one more thing, Keith. We have a new cleaner and her friend's niece has gone missing. Filipino girl, early twenties, wanted to make some money and didn't want to be a domestic for the rest of her life. Can't say I blame her but it's either a coincidence or I suspect she's been caught up in all of this—and you know how I feel about coincidences.' He paused for a moment. 'I'll email you more details. Could you find out whether she was on the boat and if so, whether or not she's survived?'

'Will do.'

'Right. I have to go, Keith. Our little discovery this morning has become more urgent and I have to speak to George now.'

'Roger that.'

'I'll contact you as soon as I have any further information, unless I hear from you first.'

Matt rushed into the kitchen when they finished the call. 'Put the news on, Elena,' he said. 'A boat's capsized in the Med and it came from Souvia. The people on it were being trafficked – sold into the slave trade.'

'Oh, no. Have they managed to save them?'

Matt shook his head as Elena switched on the television and channel hopped, hoping to find something. 'It doesn't look like the news has broken yet, Matt. Do you think Analyn's friend…?'

'I do, yes. The girl on the bondu, the discovery in the cave this morning, the missing girl; I think it's all connected, Elena. I know George is busy but I need to speak to him as soon as possible.'

Elena watched as Matt made the call. There was no answer on George's direct line, nor when Elena tried Chloe's.

'They're either out in the sticks and the signal is bad, or busy in a meeting, or interviewing. But this can't wait, Elena.' Matt phoned the station and left a message with Sergeant Demetri Lambrou, asking that George return his call as soon as possible.

'I know that George will ask Dr Kostas or Anna to get as much information from the jacket as they can, so I'm going to go there now to save some time.'

'Go where?' Elena knew the names, but couldn't remember from where.

'Forensics, Elena. I'm going to the lab.'

'Shall I come with you?'

'No. It's fine if you're happy to stay here.'

Elena nodded.

'I'll be back in a few hours. I can't sit here doing nothing when the criminals might already be trying to escape. Hopefully George will phone while I'm on the way there.'

'Okay, Matt, and if I hear anything on the news I'll give you a call.'

They said their goodbyes, Elena knowing that the more Matt thought he was helping to find the people who'd put the girl in the bondu into a coma, the less likely he was to have nightmares about the train crash.

George had ordered he wasn't to be disturbed as he reviewed the reports from the night shift, specifically the one about the boat that had left Souvia and had capsized

68

in the Mediterranean. Early indications showed that there were nine confirmed survivors, most of whom were women in their late teens or early twenties. It seemed that they were either of Eastern European or South East Asian origin. A man had also survived. George put down the papers for a moment and ran a hand through his hair. Human trafficking was still alive and thriving in twenty-first century Europe and he intended to put a stop to it, from his own country at the very least.

He picked up the report and finished reading. Now he wanted to know where the women were recruited and where the boats sailed from. People-trafficking was a lucrative business, and assuming that the organisers were greedy, George wondered if they would try to carry on at the risk of being caught, or move their operations to another country. Whatever way they decided to go, he knew the criminals would be busy trying to cover their tracks as quickly as they could, and to move any more women they planned to traffic before the survivors were interviewed and gave the game away. Time was therefore of the essence.

He took his phone out of his pocket and switched off silent mode at the same time that somebody knocked at his door.

'Doctor Kostas called, boss. He's at work and Matt Elliott has brought him a jacket found in one of the caves at Griffon's Point Beach. Matt has a theory and wants to speak to you as soon as you're free.'

'Get the car, Chloe, we're going to the forensics lab.'

Twenty minutes later they pulled up at the building and hurried inside. After signing in, Phil, the flamboyant receptionist, escorted them to Doctor Kostas's office, even though they'd been there many times before.

Kostas and Matt were talking and they stopped when George and Chloe entered the room. After quick greetings, Kostas got straight down to business. 'You know about the jacket found by Matt?'

'Yes, Kostas, thanks. What's the news?'

'We found blood on the jacket. We can tell that it's from someone who is O Positive which as you know–'

'…is the most popular blood group, so we're not going to get very far with that,' George interrupted.

'Go to the top of the class,' Kostas said, with a smile. 'But we also found some strands of hair with the follicles attached, which may indicate that violence was involved. Having been able to analyse the hair and extract the DNA, I can tell you that it came from a woman of South East Asian origin, probably from the Philippines.'

'We'll take the jacket back for Chloe to try to find out where it was bought. Thanks for your help.'

'No problems. Do they know about the card, Matt?' 'Card?'

'They will shortly,' Matt said, and explained to George and Chloe about the card that had been found with the jacket.

'The Satin and Honey Club, eh? We already know about this one. It has a clientele of exclusively rich and powerful men. If our initial investigations are correct, it looks like when the girls realise their worth and start asking for more, that's when they outlive their usefulness here and are sold on.'

'I thought exactly the same,' Matt said, 'but my views are based on assumption and not any investigations. You already know something about it?'

George explained about the issues raised by Clive Brayshaw and the investigation they'd sparked.

'I was going to update you next time we spoke, Matt, but it seems that events are moving very quickly on this case. Chloe,' he said, turning to the DS. 'Find out where this jacket was sold while I update Matt on exactly what's been going on.'

Chloe disappeared and Matt and George left the building and headed for Matt's car. George waited until they were inside and the doors were closed before speaking.

'We have intelligence that there's going to be another shipment tomorrow. Ideally, I'd like to catch them in the act but we both know it doesn't always work like that. I'm going to organise two operations – the first will be to raid the club. If we haven't discovered where they're holding the girls by tomorrow, the second team will go directly to the beach where you found the jacket. If we don't strike lucky with that, we'll have police boats manning other likely areas so that's Plan B. You'll join Chloe and I on the beach operation. Whatever happens, I want this gang closed down by close of play tomorrow, and no more lives ruined.'

Wee Jimmy turned on the music and sat quietly in the car while Janus drove. They watched the exit signs disappear one by one as they carried on along the highway, heading west towards their destination. After exiting the highway, they drove on A-roads, which eventually turned into tracks. Jimmy turned the music down and listened for any noises from the boot as Janus navigated the four-by-four SUV along the uneven track. The men were occasionally jostled when the vehicle hit a pothole or an unseen dip. All was quiet in the boot; whatever Suzy had given the girl to knock her out was working perfectly.

'Bloody typical Souvia driver,' Jimmy said, as the car bounced into a hole. 'Take it easy, I want to get there in one piece.'

Janus resisted the urge to tell his boss what he really thought of him – the money was too good for that. But as soon as he made a name for himself and got the contacts he needed, he'd start his own business and be in competition with Jimmy. Janus knew the list of people he was in contact with was almost on a par with Jimmy and, being a local, he wouldn't have to restrict himself to those who only spoke English.

'What are you smiling at?'

'Just happy to be out and about, boss.'

'Bloody weirdo,' Jimmy whispered under his breath and Janus laughed. The headlights shone alternatively towards the countryside and then out to sea as they continued the drive along the snaked track. Griffon Point was off in the distance but their destination was before that. There may have been lights on in the old, disused farmhouse, but Jimmy couldn't tell because the blackout curtains were drawn – good, somebody was doing their job properly. They kept driving along the winding track, the building looming larger as they neared. Ten bumpy minutes later, they arrived at their destination. Despite having phoned ahead, the house was quiet, everyone sleeping.

As Jimmy opened the door, the guard jumped up to his feet. His automatic weapon clattered to the ground as he did so. The sound was so loud in the still night air it could have woken the dead. The other guard was already on his feet, holding his machine gun in his arms.

Jimmy felt his heart rate quicken and the heat seemed to rise up to his face, right from his feet. They were all consciously aware of his temper as he pulled back an arm. The first punch connected with the nose of the man who had dropped his gun, and Janus flinched as he heard the bone crack. As the guard's head went back, Jimmy punched him in the stomach then kneed him in the groin. The man went down, heavily. The fury was upon him and the others watched as their colleague took a beating. The other guard knew he was next and, after the initial shock, he jumped into action. Pointing his weapon upwards, he pulled the trigger. The noise was enough to stop Jimmy in his tracks and he looked up as debris fell to the floor, exposing a hole in the ceiling.

'You stupid–' Jimmy started, and then they all turned their attention towards the closed door when they heard movement from the other side of it. Jimmy moved to the door and attempted to turn the knob. It didn't budge. He knew the girls were locked in; he'd check on them later. As he turned back, the guard with the gun was at the front door. Jimmy didn't try to stop him as he opened it and ran outside. A car started up a few seconds later and they heard it disappear into the distance.

'We have fifteen girls to control with one driver and a guard who won't be able to remember what planet he's on when he comes round, never mind his name. Good going, boss.'

'Shut up, Janus, unless you want some of the same.'

'What's your plan?' Janus asked, doing his best to keep the contempt out of his voice.

'We have plenty of time to sort this. Sit him up on a chair and if we need to let any of the girls use the bathroom, make sure they see him and the gun – but empty the magazine in case any of them get brave. That should give them an idea of what's in store if they try to escape. The gunshot will have done us a favour too. It's all quiet and they're locked in, so we have nothing to worry about for now. Get the other girl out of the boot and into the room with the rest. Then get your head down for a few hours while I make a couple of calls. By the time I wake you, there'll be two more guards on the way here. When we're ready to leave later, we'll have all the help we need.'

'And what about the one who ran away?'

'He won't get far, Janus, don't you worry about that.'

Janus said nothing further and did as he was told. The guard was coming round but was moaning and in no fit state to argue the toss. He kept slumping when Janus tried to sit him upright on one of the hard-backed chairs, so he got some string from the kitchen and tied it around the man's middle and then around to the back of the chair where he secured it, and also tied his hands. Next, he tied each of the man's ankles to the legs of the chair and stepped back to look at his handiwork. The man's head slumped forward, blood dripping from one of his nostrils.

When Jimmy started talking on the phone and went outside, Janus went to the kitchen and found a dishrag. He turned on the rusty tap and let it run for a while until the water ran clear. Wetting the cloth, he returned to the living room and listened. Jimmy was still outside talking so he took the cloth and wiped the blood from the guard's face. His nose was bent and one side of his face was already swollen. The man groaned as Janus worked around the swelling and his already bruised eye, putting slight pressure on his bent nose which stopped the bleeding. After cleaning him up, he returned to the

74

kitchen, took a bottle of water out of the fridge, and gave the man a drink. The guard guzzled the water down as quickly as he could before it started dribbling down his chin. Then Janus took the bottle away.

'Thanks, mate,' the man whispered, and Janus knew he was going to be all right, for the time being, anyway. He couldn't say what would happen to him once the man in charge discovered he'd been sleeping on the job, but the guard would remember Janus in future and was a possibility when recruiting for his new team. He was already certain that he wouldn't be caught napping on any future jobs.

Chapter 8

It was Valentine's Day and Elena's first day back at work since Matt's arrival. She woke to a delicious smell as he carried a tray up the stairs and into the bedroom.

'Smoked salmon and scrambled egg, Matt, and on a weekday.'

He leant over and kissed her. 'Enjoy, my beautiful Valentine. I'm taking Jenny out and I'll give you surprise number two on my return.'

Elena couldn't stop smiling as she tucked into her breakfast. She had initially decided to push the boat out and cook a sumptuous meal for Matt for a change as a Valentine's Day treat, instead of them eating out, but because he was now going to be working late with George, they'd agreed to delay it by one day.

She'd also bought him the latest iPhone that he'd kept meaning to buy himself but hadn't yet got around to, as a surprise. Money was easier now that the family business didn't owe Mrs Green anything. Elena recalled the meeting that Fiona Green held in the Flamingo Room; a meeting with all of her debtors, where she'd said, as a gesture of goodwill, that she was going to write-off all future debts and that they could expect to hear from her within the next few months. In the meantime, she'd handed everyone a piece of paper confirming what had been said and advising them to cancel future direct debits. It had been a fascinating meeting and still made Elena smile when she thought about it.

Elena pushed thoughts of Fiona Green to one side. The following night was going to be special. She wanted an intimate night and, work commitments permitting, planned on leaving the new assistant manager in charge and to finish early for a change.

She ate the last of her breakfast, put the tray to one side and popped into the bathroom for a quick shower. As she dried herself she heard the front door opening. Then she heard Matt's tread on the stairs, but no sound of Jenny running up them to greet Elena as if she hadn't seen her for weeks, rather than just overnight. She smiled to herself again, knowing what it meant if Matt wasn't bringing Jenny up to say good morning. The bedroom door opened and Elena dropped her towel to walk out of the bathroom.

'Is this my second surprise?' she asked.

'The only surprise is that I could keep my hands off you before I went out,' he said and kissed her.

A little while later there was scratching at the door, and then a soft bark. Matt got up to let Jenny in.

'It's a shame you have to work tonight, Matt. Your surprise will have to wait until tomorrow.' Elena sighed, sitting up in bed. 'And what's so important anyway that you've had to change your plans? Wait until I see George, I'll give him a piece of my mind.'

Knowing he couldn't share any details with Elena, Matt ignored her questions and stopped her tirade with a kiss. 'I'm sorry,' he said when they broke apart. 'I'll make it up to you, I promise.'

'Oh, I know you will, Matt,' she said, giving him a knowing look. 'It's something to do with the beach where we found that jacket isn't it? My guess is that you're hoping to catch them at it.'

'I have no idea, Elena, and I won't find out until later today,' he said, confident that his poker face would fool her and deciding that a white lie was the best way of responding. 'And anyway, you know I can't talk about official police business.'

'Fair enough. Anyway, I'd better get ready for work or I'll be late.'

'Does it matter? You're the boss.'

'Lead by example and all of that,' Elena said, giving Jenny a quick cuddle before she jumped out of bed and started to dress.

Elena blasted Kylie Minogue out of her car's music system as she drove to work, singing away as she did. Breakfast in bed, lovemaking, and a lovely bunch of red roses waiting for her in the kitchen – 'Not a bad way to start the day,' she said to herself then, 'I should be so lucky, lucky, lucky, lucky!' Singing away to Kylie, she knew that she certainly was.

Janus hurried to get the bundled girl out of the car boot and into the house. There were a few disused farmhouses dotted around the countryside within sight of theirs, and although he knew they were empty, he ensured she was fully covered by a blanket as he didn't want to give anyone the opportunity to see what he was doing, in case someone was spying on them. *Just because you're paranoid, it doesn't mean they're not out to get you,* he reminded himself as he went about his business. Although a dead weight, she wasn't a heavy woman and she groaned as he lifted her. He kicked open the door and put her on the settee, then he took the key to the room where the women were from the ledge above the door and unlocked it. Most of the women inside were lying down on the manky blankets or their own coats, huddled together either for comfort or to keep warm overnight as there was still a chill in the air. A few opened their eyes with one or two looking directly at him, but most ignored him. As he laid the woman on the floor, two of them sat up and crawled towards her. He ignored them as he watched another sit up.

'I need the toilet,' one of them said.

Janus nodded to the almost full bucket in the corner of the room.

'More than pee.'

'Bring the bucket with you,' he said, and the woman did as she was told.

He quickly locked the door and could see her eyes darting around the room firstly to Graham, and then to the gun on one of the chairs.

'I'll use it if anyone tries to escape,' Janus said, conversationally, and the girl nodded and looked down. He led her towards the back door for her to go outside and empty the bucket.

'Toilet, please,' the woman said.

He nodded and she put the bucket down and headed for the bathroom. He locked her in and not much later heard the old-fashioned chain flush and the running tap. The woman walked out of the bathroom as soon as he unlocked the door and went to the kitchen where she picked up the bucket and took it outside to empty. He watched her while she did so and when she came back into the house she washed her hands in the kitchen sink and then looked directly at Janus.

'Can we have some water please, and food, or we will be dead by the time we get to wherever you are sending us.'

He was taken aback at her bluntness, but tried not to show it. He knew his boss wouldn't get all of the money if the goods were damaged on arrival, and not fit for work almost straight away. Jimmy was still out the

79

front and it made sense to feed them now, while both he and Jimmy were awake. That way, if there was any trouble, they could both handle it. He decided to ask the boss first. Having seen what he'd done to the guard, he didn't want to be on his bad side for making the wrong decision.

'Wait here,' he said to the woman, heading for the front door to speak to Jimmy.

Rosalee couldn't believe her luck. They'd been cooped up in this old house for over twenty-four hours and if the rumours were to be believed, were going to be shipped off to God only knew where for their bodies to be used and abused, and their minds to be broken. The men hadn't put a foot wrong since their arrival but now this one had become distracted and had made his first mistake. She knew they must be in the middle of nowhere, but it made no difference to her. Thinking on her feet, she quietly opened the fridge and took out a bottle of water and one of the wrapped sandwiches. Putting the water into her pocket next to the socks she'd stored there earlier, she put the sandwich in the opposite pocket and slowly opened the back door. There was a slight squeak and Rosalee held her breath for a second, expecting the man with the gun to return and punish her. Nothing happened and she didn't hang around any longer. She was off like a gazelle being chased by a pride of lions.

Outside the front of the house, Janus was talking to Jimmy. 'The women are waking up. Some need to use the bathroom and we'll need to feed and water them. I'm happy to spend half an hour doing that now before getting my head down for a few hours, rather than you having to wake me up to do toilet escort duties.'

'I suppose it is a two-man job,' Jimmy agreed. 'I have one more call to make then we'll do it. Go back inside and get everything ready.'

As soon as he saw the bucket and the open back door, Janus knew exactly what had happened. 'Damn!' he muttered, mentally slapping himself for making such a schoolboy error. He went out the back and looked around, but couldn't see the woman anywhere. Coming back in, he looked towards the front door. New staff would be on their way shortly and Jimmy wouldn't spare him a beating, just because they were on their own. As for the girl? It was miles to the nearest town on foot, and they'd taken the women's shoes away so it would be even harder going. He estimated it would be dark by the time she covered the twenty-five miles or so and that was only if she was reasonably fit. By the time she raised the alarm they'd be long gone and the goods would be on the boat. Janus made a decision and quickly locked the back door. He grabbed the bucket and the gun that was sitting on the chair. With the bucket in one hand and the gun under his arm, he went to the bedroom and unlocked the door. Stepping inside, he put down the bucket and closed the door behind him.

He looked at each woman in the room until he saw the fear in their eyes. 'Your friend made a mistake and paid the price. Silencers are wonderful,' he added as he waved the gun around. 'I don't want the same to happen to any of you, so do exactly what I tell you, when I tell you. Understand?'

There were mutterings of agreement and nodding heads.

'Good. I'm going to bring in food and water.'

'Can I use the bathroom, please?' a woman asked in an almost begging tone.

'Come with me,' he said, and carried out the same procedure as he had with the first woman, locking the door behind them and the bathroom door while she was in there. When she knocked on the bathroom door, Janus unlocked it. He'd lined up the sandwiches and water bottles on the kitchen counter. 'Take the water,' he said. 'Distribute it amongst the others and come back for the rest of the water and the food until it's all in the room.'

She did as she was told and there was quiet for a few minutes as the women quenched their thirst and gobbled down the food. By the time one of them knocked on the door, Jimmy was back in the room and was content to sit, holding the gun, aiming it at the women as, one by one, they were allowed to use the bathroom after eating and drinking.

'The new guards will be here by the time we're ready to leave,' he said. 'And one of the boss's men will come for him,' he nodded towards the tied up guard, 'before then. Now go and get some kip.'

'Got it,' Janus said, and disappeared into another room that had a made-up bed in the corner. He had no idea who had last slept in it and didn't particularly care. Shattered after being awake for some thirty-six hours, he was sleeping as soon as his head hit the deck.

After a night at the club, Mark made his way home to the villa he shared with Grace and the boys, far enough from Griffon's Point to be away from the tourist area, but near enough to reap the benefits when they wanted.

'Mummy, I want Choco pops,' he heard Ryan saying as he put the key in the door, then the boys saw him and Ryan shouted, 'Daddy!' The six-year-old threw himself at his father and hugged him. 'You smell funny, Daddy,' he said.

His wife turned from the breakfast bar and gave him a death stare, she was already suspicious of his behaviour and was now more determined than ever to get hold of his phone and check his contacts when the opportunity arose.

Mark Junior gurgled from his high chair where their Filipino helper was spoon-feeding him some pureed fruit. Mark ignored both her and his wife.

'Hello, my other handsome boy–out of the way,' he told Analyn as he went to pick his son out of the high chair.

Mark Junior started crying and Analyn reacted. 'But, sir, he wants to finish his breakfast,' she said, and regretted it almost instantly.

Mark bent down so his eyes were level with Analyn's and his face inches from hers. 'Do not question me,' he said. 'Ever.'

'Yes, sir,' she said, moving away as he lifted the baby from the high chair. Mark Junior increased the volume of his protest. Analyn rubbed her hands together. Every inch of her being wanted to grab the baby away from his monster of a father but she knew she had to suppress those instincts, or face the consequences. Despite her fear she gave Mark a look of disdain and he took a step towards her.

'For goodness sake, Mark,' Grace said. 'You've only been home a few minutes and already you're causing chaos. Don't be cruel to the staff; you know how hard it is to find good workers and I don't want to lose this one.'

I am here, Analyn thought, *but not for much longer.* She didn't have long to go before leaving their employment and working full-time for Elena, and was looking forward to that day. In the meantime, she'd just knuckle down and try to keep out of his way when he was at home.

'Get Ryan ready for school, please,' Grace said to her, and Analyn jumped into action, glad for an excuse to get away from the horrible adults.

After getting Ryan ready and tidying Mark Junior up to go out with his mother, Analyn got on with the cleaning and started in the reception rooms. The hours she worked for the family weren't long enough to do all the jobs that needed doing, so she rotated them in order to keep on top of things. They were lazy and untidy people in the home and they really needed a full-time cleaner, probably a full-time housekeeper, Analyn thought, but they were so unkind to their staff that the workers always moved on at the earliest opportunity when they could find other work. Analyn knew that if she gave notice to leave, her life would be miserable while she worked her notice and she would be even more frightened of being alone in the house with Mr Mark – more than she already was. She'd decided on the coward's way having already planned her escape, as she thought of it, to come after her Easter pay day. A friend had agreed to phone to say that she'd been taken into hospital and wouldn't be able to come back. Unsure whether the family ever visited Elena's hotel, Analyn didn't work as front of house there so there was no concern that she might bump into them. Even if she did, he would only make himself look bad if he berated her in public and Elena wouldn't stand for that.

Now that was sorted, Analyn cleared her mind of any problems or worries and got stuck into her work. Mr Fletcher was in bed and Mrs Fletcher and the boys had left the house. Quiet as she could be, she cleaned most of downstairs before eventually ending up in the kitchen.

Analyn noticed a phone on the breakfast bar – it was black and didn't have any jewels hanging from it, so she knew that it belonged to Mr Mark. He always took his phone upstairs with him when he went to bed and she wondered if he'd forgotten it or whether he didn't want to be disturbed. Knowing he could switch it to silent, she thought the former. As he was an accountant by trade, she also wondered why he stayed out working all night. She shook her head: it was none of her business and there was no way she was going to disturb him by taking his phone to him. She was already being careful not to make too much noise and she didn't have any music on, like she usually did when the whole family was out. Mr Mark was like a bear in hibernation when he slept after a nightshift, and the last thing she wanted was for that bear to wake up before he was ready.

The phone was like a magnet and she wondered what information it held, and if the rumours in her community were true. She had already looked through the house when the family had been out as a favour to Gloria, but hadn't found anything apart from discovering a safe behind the biggest picture on the bedroom wall, but Analyn assumed this was normal for rich people. Something wasn't right with this family and she was glad to be able to leave the Fletcher family employment, and grateful for the opportunities Elena had given her.

The granite kitchen surfaces glistened by the time she'd finished in the kitchen and Analyn was about to start on the floors when she heard his phone buzz and light up at the same time. She read the words, *URGENT Fletch I need to sp...* before the light went out. Analyn wondered who wanted to speak to him and who would dare to bother him, especially if the person knew he had worked the night before and would probably be sleeping. Brave man, she thought, making another assumption that it was a man. The tinny sound of Right Said Fred's *I'm too Sexy...* filled the silence and she almost jumped out of her skin at the ring tone. Without thinking of the consequences, she grabbed the phone. The caller ID said 'office', and Analyn pressed the green answer icon.

'Fletch, it's Jimmy. I've just heard the boat capsized and if anyone's survived they'll be on to us.' He was breathless and rushing his words. 'What about tonight's shipment. What do you want me to...Are you there, Fletch? Fletch?'

Analyn pressed the red icon to terminate the call. Then she dropped the phone onto the breakfast bar as if it were on fire. She put her left hand to her mouth and tapped her nails against her teeth, wondering what to do. She heard movement from upstairs and the phone rang again. Then she did the same as she had every other time she had a crisis in her life. She touched the beads around her neck and then squeezed the cross.

'Lord help me, please.' she whispered. Then, knowing she didn't have much time, she grabbed her bag from the breakfast bar stool and left quietly via the back door. Analyn ran down the driveway, out of the gates and down the hill towards the town. She jumped on the first bus that stopped and alighted when it arrived in the centre of Griffon's Point. Rushing into the Mall, she took her phone out of her bag and made a call.

It had been a busy day so far and, as Matt was working that night, Elena decided to go home, take Jenny out, then to return to the hotel that evening. They offered a three-course Valentine's day meal and had booked a local singer to serenade the lovers while they enjoyed their dinner. The service was fully booked so Elena had decided to help out, even though she knew her staff had it covered and could manage well enough without her. Her phone rang as she drove out of her parking space and she pressed the hands-free button on the steering wheel and answered.

'Mrs Elena, help me.' It was Analyn and she sounded terrified.

Elena parked up, wanting to give her full attention to the call. 'Analyn, whatever is the matter?'

'I'm really sorry to bother you, Mrs Elena, but I think I'm in trouble and I need your help.'

'What's happened, Analyn? Has somebody hurt you? Are you safe?'

'Not yet, Mrs Elena, but they might not be when they find out what I know. I'm safe for now.' Analyn looked around. Local people were coming and going about their business and they wouldn't know what she was talking about, but she wasn't willing to risk it. 'I can't tell you on the phone. Can you help me?'

'Where are you?'

She explained where she was and Elena told her she'd be there as soon as she could.

Parking up where Analyn had said she would be, Elena had a quick look around, frowning when she couldn't see her. About to get back into her car, she heard a voice.

'Mrs Elena.' Elena looked around and saw Analyn appear from behind a stack of bags, purses and wallets, under the canopy of one of the shops.

'Good grief, Analyn, I nearly missed you,' Elena said, noting that the woman was looking around like a hunted animal. 'Come on, get into the car and you can tell me all about it.'

'Are you on your own?' Analyn asked, and rushed around to the passenger seat when Elena said she was.

'I've done something very bad,' Analyn said as Elena started driving them towards her home.

'What's happened?'

'The family I work for, they are...' She hesitated, trying to find the right words in a language that was sometimes hard for her to understand. 'The wife can be uncaring and treats me like a servant. I can live with that because it's only her words that can hurt me and I have become used to that. But the husband—' She closed her eyes and shook her head for a second. 'He is a very bad man and he frightens me. He has threatened me a few times and I try not to be alone with him.'

'Oh, Analyn, that's terrible! Why didn't you tell me before? You must leave there, immediately.

'I have left, but not in the way I expected to. Mr Mark came in from his night shift and when Mrs Grace left with the children he went to bed. That's how I like it. They are all out of the way and I can get on with my work without fear or hassle. But I noticed he left his phone in the kitchen and I couldn't help myself. When his phone buzzed I looked at it.'

'And?'

'And, it said *Fletch*. That's the nickname the man used for him because his surname is Fletcher.'

'Fletcher?' Elena asked. 'Mark Fletcher?'

'That's right, yes. So–'

'I know a Mark Fletcher. But he's an accountant, or he was, anyway,' Elena interrupted, wondering if there could be another Mark Fletcher on the island. It wasn't an uncommon name in the U.K. but what were the chances? And if it was the same man, he was as sleazy as his former boss.

'His boss died and I heard Mrs Grace saying to a friend that he was going to–' Analyn stopped for a second as she tried to recall the right word. '…going to diversify, or something like that. But, Mrs Elena, his phone rang and I couldn't help myself. I answered it and a man called Jimmy said that a boat had capsized and that if anyone talked they'd be onto them. He also asked him what to do about tonight's shipment.'

'And what did you say when you heard all of this?'

'I ended the call and put the phone down. The phone rang again, Mrs Elena, and I didn't know what to do. Then I heard Mr Mark moving about upstairs and I knew I'd be in big trouble when he found out I answered his phone, so I got the hell out of there.'

Elena let out an inappropriate laugh at the Filipino's use of the phrase and Analyn looked at her, eyes wide and mouth agape. 'This is funny?'

'No, of course not, just the way you said… I'm sorry, Analyn, never mind. What we have to do now is get you to safety and then call the police. We're going to my home and you'll be safe there.'

'Thanks, Mrs Elena, but no to the police. They never take complaints from people like me seriously and won't believe me over Mr Mark. He'll cover his tracks and as soon as he finds out what I've done he'll come looking for me. If he thought I'd been to the police, I could be the next person to go missing.'

'But that won't happen, Analyn, I'll help you.'

'I'm not going to the police now,' Analyn said. 'I'm frightened but I can't go on like this. I'm going to try to find out more information, get more evidence, and then then when I go to the police they will have to believe me.'

The determined look on Analyn's face told Elena that she wouldn't be able to change her mind. She remained quiet for a few moments as she started putting two and two together and wondered if what she had in mind might work. Matt wouldn't be happy with what she was planning, but he had put himself out of contact for the time being and this was urgent.

They pulled up at the house and Analyn followed Elena inside. Jenny and Elena greeted each other and Analyn watched for a few moments before Elena gestured for her to sit down. Keen to meet the new visitor, Jenny sat in front of her, looking adorable. When that didn't work, the dog gently pawed Analyn's knee and the woman eventually gave the dog a tentative pat on the head. When Jenny responded with a thump of her tail, Analyn became more confident and stroked her, waiting for Elena to speak.

'I'll make some tea then we'll talk about the best way to handle this.'

'I'll help.'

'It's okay, Analyn, I'll do it. You stay there with Jenny. Milk or lemon?'

'Milk please, and no sugar,' Analyn said, as Elena disappeared into the kitchen.

She returned with two mugs and a plate of biscuits. After taking a bite out of a chocolate digestive, Elena gave Analyn a thoughtful look. 'I might be able to help you with this,' she said. 'We found a jacket in the caves at the far end of Griffon's Point Beach. Matt took it to the police forensic lab to be analysed. There was blood on it, Analyn, and a card fell out of the pocket. A card with the name of a so-called gentlemen's club on it. Satin and Honey something.'

'I've heard Mr Mark talk about a club, but he's never named it, just said *The Club*. I wonder if–'

'It could be a coincidence and we're barking up the wrong tree, or–'

Analyn gave her a curious look.

'It means I could be putting two and two together and coming up with…what it means is that we could be assuming that he's involved and that it's the same club, but we are wrong and he has nothing to do with it.'

'I doubt that very much. He is guilty into his eyeballs. Sorry, *up* to his eyeballs I mean, and I think it all fits. If he is in charge of a club and is employing girls and then sending them away, God only knows what's happened to Gloria's niece Rosalee, and any others.' She clasped the cross hanging around her neck and closed her eyes. Hoping to get strength from it, Elena assumed.

Chapter 9

Rosalee kept off the main track and ran like the clappers. There was a hedgerow adjacent to the track and she knew that if she reached it she could stop for a minute and be out of sight of anyone who might be looking for her from the old building. Ignoring the pain in her feet as they hit pebbles or sharp grasses, she kept going. As soon as she reached cover, Rosalee slumped to the ground. She brushed the mess off the bottom of her feet and pulled out a death star – the slang name for the spiky dried bud that grew on bondu cacti and caused grief to humans and animals alike – which had embedded itself into the sole of her foot. She put on her socks, resisted the urge to take a drink of water, and started running again, as fast as she could. She had no idea how long she'd been going, but when she stopped again to catch her breath, she turned to look towards the farmhouse. She could still see it, but it was just a small blot on the landscape.

She couldn't believe what had happened to her and her friends. She was also amazed that she'd escaped – for the moment – and that nobody seemed to be following her. Rosalee rued the day she'd listened to a friend and had decided to sell her body in exchange for a better standard of living. Some of the girls thought their treatment was God's punishment in return for their sins, but if that was the case, Rosalee thought, how would God punish the evil men who were trafficking and selling the women for use as sex slaves? She had no doubt that's what they would be used for.

The socks had helped but her feet were still stinging from pounding along the hard ground. She took a drink of water and, doing her best to ignore the pain, ran at full speed again, knowing that her life and those of others depended on her getting to safety. Keeping adjacent to the track the vehicle had come along when they were brought to the building, she carried on like this, sprinting, slowing down to a jog, and then resting when she could go no further.

The men had taken most of their belongings from them, including their phones and watches, so the only idea Rosalee had of the time was the sun's journey from East to West. It was starting to go down as she noticed a building off in the distance, and heard the sound of bells. Not much later, she heard an engine approaching and then the vehicle was almost upon her. Exhausted, she still managed to jump to one side as an open topped buggy went past, the man driving, occasionally checking behind him. She quickly realised that other vehicles were following.

'Eee ha!' shouted a man driving the next vehicle and the woman sitting beside him gave her a wave. Four others followed, and by the time she realised these were tourists out on a jolly and shouted for help, they were long gone. Running on pure adrenaline, and using every ounce of strength she had left, Rosalee upped her momentum and headed in the direction they were driving. Again she heard the sound of bells, but this time it was closer and a small herd of goats appeared from over a hill. There was no immediate sign of their herder, but when he came into view she could see that he was just a young boy.

'Can you help me?' she asked. 'Do you have a phone?'

The boy turned and ran away. Out of steam and the water long finished, it was sheer determination and concern for the safety of her friends that carried Rosalee's legs onwards. Shortly after there was a bend in the track she was now on and she could see a building in the distance. The buggies were parked outside and their sight gave her the oomph she needed.

The people stopped talking about their fun day out over the Souvia countryside when they saw the woman stagger into the café's patio area.

'Are you all right, love?' asked the woman who had waved at her from the buggy passenger seat.

Rosalee collapsed to the ground, put her head in her hands and cried.

While another team were carrying out a raid at the club, George, Matt, and Chloe were in the armoured mini bus with another section of the armed police team, heading in the direction of the old farmhouse that Rosalee had told the police about. As soon as details of the call had been passed to all stations in Souvia, Sergeant Demetri Lambrou had picked up on it and informed the DCI. Knowing that time was of the essence, George mounted the operation and immediately changed plans from the beach to the farmhouse, knowing it would be easier to contain. Rosealee had given enough information for them to be able to track her journey backwards from the café she had run to. As they headed towards the old farmhouse, George had the sinking feeling that they were going to find it deserted. On arrival, his fears were confirmed.

'Secure the building,' George said to the sergeant in charge of the eight-man team, 'and radio as soon as…'

'…it's clear. Yes, Sir, will do,' she replied. She opened the back doors of the mini-bus and George, Matt, and Chloe watched as she spoke quietly to her team, giving them hand signals of where she wanted them to go. Less than a few minutes later, when part of the team were around the back of the farmhouse, those at the front battered the doors down and entered the house.

'Secure, Sir,' came the call. 'Nobody here, but we've got signs that there was. An unflushed toilet, dirty cups, cigarette ends, and a piece of paper with 'help us' written on it.'

'Roger that,' George replied, before leaving the mini-bus with Matt and Chloe and entering the building.

'As we thought,' Matt said.

'They've probably cancelled their journey,' Chloe said. George and Matt looked at each other.

'What?' she asked.

'These gangs are motivated by nothing but greed,' Matt said. 'And the temptation might just be too great. I have a feeling about this.'

'Me too,' George replied.

He wasn't the only one who had a feeling, and as Analyn's story unfolded, Elena kept thinking about the jacket and card they'd found in the cave at Griffon's Point Beach. She smiled as she watched Jenny sitting with her head on Analyn's lap. It had been clear by her initial reaction of a tentative pat on the dog's head that Analyn wasn't particularly comfortable with animals, but she'd soon realised that Jenny meant her no harm, and now seemed to take comfort from stroking and petting the dog. *It's like Jenny knows something's wrong,* Elena thought, before quickly bringing herself back to the present.

'Give me a few minutes, Analyn, while I try to get hold of Matt.'

'I have to go into hiding, Mrs Elena. If Mr Mark catches me he will kill me for sure. But first, I need to stop him from taking the girls away. Can you help me Mrs Elena?'

'Of course I can help you. Let me phone the police.'

'Not the police, Mrs Elena. I don't want to get into trouble.'

'You won't get into trouble, Analyn. I'll speak to Matt who works with the police but isn't a Souvia policeman.' *Or to my cousin George, who is,* she thought. Out loud she said, 'Please just trust me.'

Analyn chewed a nail as she looked at her, and Elena knew the woman was taking a massive leap of faith to put all of her trust in her. Saying that, Analyn thought she was on the run from a gangster who would, at the very least, give her a good hiding if he caught her. Her family was thousands of miles away and her friends didn't have the wherewithal to help, so she didn't have much choice in the matter.

After trying both Matt and George and being diverted to their message service, Elena called Chloe. She had the same result and figured they were still out on their undercover job, or whatever it was they were doing. Then the penny dropped and she remembered her conversation with Matt that morning, and his reaction.

'They're already on their way there!' she said, louder than she intended and Jenny barked and did a few twirls.

'On their way where, Mrs Elena? I don't understand.'

'To the caves, Analyn.'

Analyn put her head to one side giving Elena a questioning look.

'The caves on Griffon's Point Beach where the girls are going to be smuggled from. Matt and I found a jacket and a card there and the police are investigating. They must have found out the same information that you have and they're going to stop them. Come on, let's go.'

Analyn re-thought her decision about contacting the authorities. 'But don't you think you should call someone, just in case? What if you're–'

'It'll be fine, Analyn. Trust me, please. And we might be able to discover whether your friend's niece is there.'

Analyn wavered, but then sat back down and folded her arms. 'I'm not moving unless you call for help.'

Elena tutted as she looked at the woman who, a few minutes earlier, was telling her to get a shift on and asking her not to call the police. She raised her eyebrows but made the call anyway, and as she expected, it went straight to the automated answering service, telling her to leave a message or to call back later.

'Matt, it's me, but you already know that. I know you can't speak just now because you're at the caves or on your way there. Analyn's with me and we'll see you there. Call me as soon as you get this message, please. Love you.' She pressed the button to end the call. 'Satisfied?'

Analyn nodded and got up.

'Where's Jenny?' Elena asked. They both looked around but couldn't see the dog. 'She must be upstairs. Come on, let's go.'

As Elena began the drive out of town, a head popped up between the seats and Jenny let out a gentle bark to inform them of her presence.

'How did you get into the car?' Elena asked, and took her hand off the gear stick to find its way to the dog's soft fur to give her a pat. 'That's naughty, Jenny,' she said, then glanced at Analyn. 'But she's here now and I'm not turning around to take her back.'

They drove on in silence, but Elena noticed that Analyn frequently reached behind her to stroke Jenny.

As they neared their destination, it occurred to Elena that the car headlights could be seen for miles in the dark of the night. There were no other vehicles about and she knew the area well but even with the light from the moon, it would be suicide attempting to drive without lights on the top of the cliff. She stopped the car. 'They will probably have somebody on lookout,' she said, 'so we walk from here.'

'But we're at the top of the cliff!'

'I know. We walk until we come to the end and then there's a pathway down which will take us to the caves. This is the only way we can do it without causing suspicion if somebody's looking.'

'But if we can't see where we're going and we lose our footing…we could fall and die, Mrs Elena!'

'It's not completely dark, Analyn, and we can use the moonlight to guide us. It's a simple choice; we announce our presence with torchlight and risk being caught, or we tread carefully. Jenny's senses are better than ours and she can lead us. And anyway, by the time we get down there, Matt and the police should have arrived so we'll be safe then.'

'But what if they haven't?'

'Well, that's the exact reason why we're being cautious. If they haven't arrived yet we don't want to give ourselves away and risk being seen by the kidnappers. Do we?'

Analyn didn't answer. Elena started walking towards the pathway at the edge of the cliff. Analyn followed. Jenny ran in front of the women, keeping ahead but turning every so often and returning to the women before running ahead again–neither realised that the dog was herding them. Before too long, they arrived on the beach near the caves.

'They're not here yet,' Elena whispered, surprised that Matt and the police hadn't arrived yet. She couldn't see anyone as they headed towards the caves but knew that meant nothing. 'We have to be careful,' she added. 'And no talking from here. Stay by my side and if you hear or see anything, squeeze my arm. Understand?'

'Of course,' Analyn said, nodding her agreement. 'But what about the dog?'

'Jenny, heel,' Elena said, and the dog circled Elena, then stood on her right, walking close to her side. Analyn seemed satisfied and they walked quietly on the sand, approaching the caves. Their eyes were now fully adjusted to the night light and the moon lit up the beach as it cast its glow along the sand and into the sea. As they neared the caves, Analyn squeezed Elena's arm. 'Listen,'

Elena did as she was told but heard nothing, and looking at Analyn, she shrugged.

'I can hear an engine.'

When Elena concentrated on listening again, she could hear the distant thrum of a boat's engine. It must still have been a way off as neither could see anything as they looked out to sea.

Surprised to find nobody in the caves, the two women carried on walking in silence–a silence that was broken by the dulcet tones of Kylie Minogue singing *I should be so lucky, lucky, lucky, lucky.* Jenny barked.

'Crappity crap!' Elena swore, as she fished her phone out of her pocket and pressed the answer button, trying, at the same time, to reduce the volume.

As she did so, another voice appeared out of the darkness. 'Well, well, well. What have we here? Put the phone down.' A man was walking towards them with a gun pointing in their direction.

Elena bit her lip and held the phone out in front of her. She heard Analyn whispering to God for help, her fingers moving to her necklace, and Jenny growled a warning at the man, but stayed by Elena's side.

'Drop your phone onto the sand,' the man said. When Elena hesitated, he added, 'Do you want me to make you?' He flicked a switch on the weapon, pointing it directly at her chest.

Trying her best not to pee her pants, Elena held the phone out in front of her and dropped it.

'Dear Lord Jesus,' Analyn said. 'Save our souls from…'

'I would wait until you're out at sea before you ask for his help,' the man said without a shred of humour or compassion. 'Now come with me.' He put his gun over his shoulder and turned in the direction he'd come from.

In the vehicle with the team after leaving the farmhouse, Matt resisted the urge to call Elena's name, knowing that she was in trouble up to her ears. He thought he'd heard a dog growl in the background but couldn't be sure. The only thing he was sure of was that Elena needed to be saved.

'Put your foot down,' he called to the driver. 'We need to get to Griffon Point Beach, ASAP.'

The driver glanced to his sergeant who was sitting in the passenger seat, and all other eyes turned to Matt. He wanted to scream 'just do it!' but knew he had to be rational and explain properly for them to be able to save Elena and to catch the traffickers. 'Listen,' he said, and played the message Elena had left him. 'When I just called her she couldn't talk to me and I heard a man's voice telling her to drop her phone onto the sand, and another woman praying for help in the background.'

'Did Elena say anything?' George asked.

Matt shook his head.

'The beach. Now!' George called, taking his phone out of his pocket and calling the operations headquarters.

Without saying a word, the driver did as he was told, heading for the beach as quickly as he could drive over the bumpy track.

Elena looked to Analyn knowing they'd have a better chance of escape if they only had to tackle one man, rather than a whole boat crew. She also knew it was only a matter of time before Matt and the police arrived.

The women were being held further along the beach, instead of in the cave as Elena had expected. She was grateful that the phone signal had been good enough for Matt to get through to her, but looking around, she didn't have much else to be grateful for. The man with the gun walked in front of them as if unconcerned that they would try to get away, though he did turn around every few seconds.

His phone rang, and Elena noticed that it was an old-fashioned, small black one when he took it out of his pocket. He turned to face away from them for a few seconds, whispering into his phone. Elena looked at Analyn and put a finger to her lips. Then she turned her head slightly and inclined it behind her. Analyn had no doubt of what Elena was planning but shook her head vigorously. Her eyes were open wider than usual and she looked like a swimmer who had seen a shark heading directly for her.

Elena didn't think twice. She turned and ran, Jenny trotting along by her side. Analyn knew she had no choice and legged it after her. Their guard turned and saw what was happening. He didn't seem overly concerned as he said something into his phone and then hung up. When he'd finished talking, he didn't chase them–instead, he walked in the direction of the women prisoners and their guards, looking out to sea as the boat now came into view.

They two women ran past the caves and were almost at the bottom of the path. Elena thought they'd made it. The only sound was their panting as they ran as fast as they could. The sound of a gunshot brought them to a halt, and a man appeared at the bottom of the path, pointing his pistol at them.

Without warning, Jenny leaped through the air. Another shot rang out and Jenny yelped as she hit the man's chest, the momentum of the dog making the man fall over, with Jenny on top of him.

'Run and get help!' Elena screamed at Analyn.

This time, she only had to be told once. She took off up the path as fast as her small legs would allow. Whatever happened, Elena knew she couldn't leave Jenny and her fear disappeared momentarily as she felt a surge of love for the dog, quickly followed by bloody fury, knowing the man had shot their dog. As he struggled, Jenny was rolled to one side and Elena saw that her front left paw was covered in blood. The dog tried to get up but the pain showed in her eyes. Elena bit her lip and tried to calm herself. Turning her back to the man, she whispered, 'Play dead,' to Jenny. Jenny didn't have to do much playing as she closed her eyes, and lay deathly still.

Everything else cleared from Elena's mind when she stood up straight and looked from the man to the pistol. The gun was laying a few metres in front of where she was standing and the man was laying. He looked to where she was looking and then their eyes locked in mutual understanding.

Believing she had the advantage, Elena moved to cover the short distance. One leg did as her brain ordered but she was suddenly stopped and forced to face-plant onto the hard ground as he grabbed her left ankle and caused her to fall.

Elena tried to ignore the pain on the left side of her face and body as she attempted to crawl towards the pistol which was just out of her reach. His hand felt like a vice around her ankle and didn't budge as she tried shaking her leg to move it. Then she kicked out as hard as she could with her right foot, hoping to hurt him enough for him to move his hand.

'You little bitch!' he yelled, as he yanked her leg and pulled her further away from the pistol. He let go of her for a second as he jumped to his feet and Elena moved forward. But it wasn't enough as the man bent and pulled her back again, before moving to the pistol and picking it up.

'On your feet,' he said, pointing the pistol at her, and she wondered how such a small man could be so strong.

'You pathetic excuse for a man,' she said, as she got to her feet.

He laughed. 'You'll have enough time to think of how pathetic I am when you're on the boat. We won't get as much for you as we have for the young ones, but they'll find some use for you. Our client likes to tame the feisty ones, and I'm sure he'll enjoy—'

Ignoring the gun, Elena lunged towards the man and slapped his face. He didn't see it coming and stepped back in surprise. Recovering quickly, he lifted the pistol and swung it. Elena saw it coming and tried to dodge it, but it still caught the side of her head and she called out in pain and put a hand to her head. She felt the wetness of the blood through her hair. Looking at the man, she summed up her situation, acknowledging for the first time that she was in a bit of trouble. She had no doubt that the evil little git would use the gun again and that she had tried his patience. Self-preservation kicked in and Elena knew she would have to carry out his orders whether she liked it or not.

'Get going,' he said, and a poke in her back from the pistol encouraged her to move.

Holding the side of her head with one hand, Elena started moving, holding her breath and hoping with all her might that Jenny would stay put. After a few steps, she knew the dog was either still playing dead as Elena had told her to do, or worse still, the evil little man had killed her. She gave herself a mental shake. Despite her earlier thoughts, she couldn't change her nature and her stubbornness and sense of fair play refused to let him have all his own way. Playing for time, she limped forward as slowly as she thought she could get away with, and he didn't question why she was limping.

For the second time that night a sound came out of nowhere and filled the quiet night. She literally jumped when she heard the noise of her car horn, and the small man turned to look upwards towards the sound.

'That's the police arrived and they're coming to get you,' she said conversationally.

'Yup. Undercover police always notify their presence by blowing their horns,' he said. 'Get moving.' He nudged her with the pistol again and Elena limped forward. But as she watched him out of the corner of her eye, she could see him looking towards the top of the cliff every now and then, scanning the area for police, she hoped. He made a quick call on his phone and the only words Elena heard him say were, 'Sort it.'

A few minutes later, the horn stopped. She wondered whether Analyn had been caught again or if she'd decided to make a run for it, or indeed, risk driving the car. They were almost with the group of people now and Elena did a quick head count, believing there were about twenty people there, including another three armed men. She knew she had no chance of escape unless someone came to rescue them. For the first time, a small doubt entered her head and she wondered if she'd got it wrong and Matt and the police might not come.

'We have more cargo,' her captor told the others, who looked from him to Elena.

'She's not exactly what the man ordered is she?' Janus said, 'Unless they have grab-a-granny nights.'

The men laughed and Elena gave them a death stare.

'Bet she's a feisty one.'

'Remember this night and the choices you made when you're rotting in your prison cells,' Elena said. 'Especially you.' She turned to Wee Jimmy, the man who'd pistol-whipped her. 'Imagine the fun those big bad men can have with a little fellow like you. You'll be their little plaything, to do with as they please.'

The other men laughed and so did the women. The little man's face reddened and Elena was ready for the violence this time as he swung for her. She successfully dodged his blow, managing to avoid contact, and then did a little side-step and ran behind one of the other guards.

'Stop laughing or I'll give you a proper hiding once we've got rid of this lot,' Wee Jimmy said to his team. 'And gag that bitch. If I hear another word from her, I'll forget about any extra money and put a bullet through her head myself.' He could see the amusement in the eyes of Janus and the other guards so singled one out. Jimmy put his pistol down the back of his jeans and approached the man. 'Think it's funny when little bitches like that take the mick do you?'

The man shook his head. 'No, Jimmy, I…' He doubled over in pain when Jimmy's fist connected with his stomach. 'Now gag her and get them to the sea. Here's the boat.'

Elena and the other women watched as the boat they'd seen at a distance now seemed to grow in front of their eyes as it neared the shore, its engine getting louder as it almost finished its inward journey. She closed her eyes and tried not to gag as one of the guards put a piece of cloth – she thought it was an old scarf – into her mouth. It stank of nicotine, stale perfume, and something else that she didn't recognise. *If Matt doesn't save me I'll probably die of an infection,* she thought briefly, trying not to throw up or kill herself choking.

They were put into single file and pushed towards the sea, their armed guards on each side of them doing their best to stop anyone from escaping. It didn't work as one woman made a run for it, and didn't stop when a warning shot was fired. The other women watched as she ran as fast as she could on the hard sand in a zig zag fashion, giving her a better chance to avoid the bullets.

'Finish it,' the little man said to the man who'd fired his gun, but then they all stopped as they heard the sound of a second engine, and turned towards it. Another boat came from around the bay and sped towards the shore. It was lit up with flashing lights, and as it neared, Elena and the others could clearly see that the passengers were armed police. She gave the small man a smug look, but that soon disappeared when she saw the expression on his face. Without any words being spoken she knew without a doubt that he'd singled her out for punishment.

The driver of the boat meant to transport the women tried to turn it in an attempt to make their escape. They were too near to the shore and were easily overcome by some of the armed police who jumped out of their own boat and secured that of the criminals. The other police headed to the party on the shore. Then it seemed like the whole beach lit up and they heard a voice coming through a megaphone.

'Drop your weapons and raise your hands.'

The women huddled together as most of the men dropped their guns. But the small man hesitated and looked directly at Elena.

'Oh lordy lord,' she said as he lifted his pistol and aimed it directly at her.

As well as the police heading towards the group from the shore, another party ran along the beach and Matt was at the front of this group. Elena felt like she had tunnel vision; she was focussed on the small man and the pistol, now aimed at her head.

'I might rot in a prison cell, but you'll be rotting in hell,' he said, and Elena's world went into slow motion.

It seemed to her that Matt appeared in mid-air out of nowhere. The small man saw Elena's eyes move to look past him and his head turned slightly as he started to squeeze the trigger. The next thing Elena knew was an agonising pain in her foot and she collapsed onto the sand. The shooter was now lying face down on the sand with Matt on top of him. Matt's knee was on the man's back, and he pushed the man's face into the sand. Unable to breathe, Jimmy struggled but Matt gave him no quarter. Two armed police arrived; one took the pistol and the other lifted Jimmy's head.

Jimmy spat sand out of his mouth and screamed, 'Police brutality!' as the police pulled him to his feet, cuffed him and led him away.

Matt's concern for Elena outweighed his need to throttle her aggressor and he jumped up and rushed to her. A policeman was already with her, lifting her into a sitting position, while another was talking into her radio.

'I knew you'd come,' Elena said, leaning into Matt.

Matt took one look at Elena's foot and shouted at the uniformed officers, 'Medic! Medic! We need some help here!' then he eased her gently down onto the sand.

'They're on the way,' one of the uniforms said.

'Matt, never mind me. Get Jenny. He shot her too and I told her to play dead, but I'm not sure if she was playing or not. I'm sorry, Matt, I didn't want her to come with us but she was already in the car and I thought you'd be at the beach and that we could help you and…'

'It's going to be all right, Elena,' he said, to reassure her, trying to hide the concern from his face as he looked at her mangled foot. 'Let's get you sorted. Jenny's been through some tough times and I'm sure she'll come through this.'

'Can you give me a bit of space,' the medic said.

Now that she was safe, the adrenaline running through her body dispersed and Elena felt the intense pain. She cried out in agony as the medic gave her a shot of morphine.

'Please, Matt,' Elena said. 'Get Jenny to the vet. I'll never forgive myself if–' She closed her eyes and the medic looked at Matt.

'We need to get her to hospital and operate on her as soon as we can, to remove the bullet and stop any infection, and to check out that head wound. She's in safe hands now and will be fine.'

'I'll come with you,' Matt said.

'The quickest way is by air ambulance and there's no room, sorry. Here it is now.' he added, pointing to the helicopter. 'We'll see you there and I suggest you get your dog the treatment she needs because that's the last thing Elena thought about before going to sleep and it'll be the first thing on her mind when she comes round. She's lost some blood but it's not life-threatening and she's going to be fine.'

Knowing that Elena was now safe and there was nothing else he could do for her for the time being, Matt rushed to find Jenny. Elena's car wasn't in the car park at the west side of the beach when they'd arrived earlier, so he'd rightly assumed she must have parked it at the top of the cliff and walked down the path. He took his phone out of his pocket and called Chloe who was with the team in that area.

'I was just about to give you a call,' she said, and confirmed that Elena's car was where he'd suspected. 'Analyn is with the car and she's badly shaken up. And two of the constables have found your dog. She's been shot in the paw, and I've used a scarf as a temporary bandage, but we need to get her to the emergency vet. The problem is separating Analyn from Jenny. She's got one hand on the cross on her rosary and the other cuddling the dog, and she doesn't want to let go.'

Matt knew that feeling and acknowledged to himself that Jenny was unwittingly saving someone else, once again.

Epilogue

Matt, Elena, and Jenny were at home. Matt put down his phone after speaking to George and made some tea. As he walked into the lounge, Elena lifted herself up on the reclined side of the settee and tested her heavily bandaged foot.

'Ouch,' she said, as Matt placed her lemon tea down on the side table next to her. She winced with the pain her actions had caused.

'Well try to keep still then.'

Lying next to Elena, Jenny lifted her bandaged paw and cried. Her people parents smiled indulgently.

'Yes, we see you and know you've got a poorly foot, too,' Matt said, and then gave Jenny some attention. Satisfied, the dog put her head back on Elena's lap, closed her eyes, and was snoring softly within a minute.

'That was George on the phone. The international authorities are involved in this investigation which may take some time to unravel but we already know there are people involved here, the U.K. and Italy.'

'What will happen to that evil little man, and to Mark Fletcher? And will Fiona Green end up in prison?'

'Both the U.K. and Italy want to extradite that evil little man who's known as Wee Jimmy Wilson, and he will go down for a very long time, Elena.'

'Wee Jimmy Wilson? He didn't sound very Scottish.'

'I'm told he lived in Scotland for a while, but is originally from Essex. Apparently, he wanted to portray a hard-man, Glasgow image, but couldn't do the accent.'

'That's pathetic and he seemed nasty enough without pretending to be something else.'

'Small man syndrome, I guess. He will end up in prison, but the question is where. Because both countries want him we'll have to see what happens. My guess is that he'll be extradited to the U.K. As far as Mark Fletcher is concerned, they caught him trying to escape with his assistant; a woman called Suzy who was the madam for want of a better word. I feel sorry for his poor wife who didn't know about his dealings apparently. Two young kids, too.'

'It's a shame, but I still hope he's locked away for a very long time.'

'It's going to take a while to unpick everything, but my guess is that Mark Fletcher will spend his time in prison in Souvia, and so will Suzy.' Seeing the look of concern on Elena's face, he added. 'They'll all be kept locked up until that happens along with the other men involved, so you have nothing to worry about.'

'That's good to know.'

'As for Fiona Green, she asked for help as soon as she smelt a rat. These activities may have gone on for some time longer, had her lawyer not taken the action that he did. She won't be charged or go to prison.'

'The foundation she set up is going to help the victims so at least something good has come out of this, Matt.'

'I agree. And I'm told the Fig Tree Foundation is already providing accommodation for some of the women, with trained counsellors to help them, too.'

'Really? Well that's good to hear, Matt.'

'How's Analyn?'

'She phoned earlier and is feeling much better. She said she doesn't want a whole week off and wants to return to work tomorrow – if she's busy she doesn't over think things and she just wants to get back to normal. Her words, Matt, not mine. She told me that Rosalee, the girl who ran from the farmhouse and raised the alarm, is the niece of her friend Gloria. She also said that Rosalee is going to have some sort of liaison role in the Fig Tree Foundation and has already moved to that accommodation. You know, from what she's done and the way she's acted since her husband died, it's like Fiona Green's had a personality transplant.'

'Major events can change a person's outlook on life and make them question how they live it.'

Elena nodded at Matt's response. 'So much for a leopard never changing its spots. But the Education Minister clearly couldn't. His fall from grace is all over social media and the news.'

'Indeed, and he's another one who can expect a long prison sentence, and the fact that he's rich won't make it any easier for him.'

They both drank their tea in silence, reflecting on the recent events.

Matt broke the silence, looking forward to telling Elena about his daughter. 'On a happier note, I have some other news.'

Elena finished her tea and waited.

'Kayleigh messaged. She's going to phone later, but she's been offered a job here for the season with Aphrodite Adventures, and her boyfriend's coming too.'

'Oh that's great news, Matt. I get to meet Kayleigh at long last and her boyfriend. And we'll be able to spend some time together.'

'It is great news. She wants to see us as soon as they arrive and before starting work. The company will put them up in an apartment and she's going to tell me all about it when she calls later.'

'This is just what we need, Matt. We seem to have moved from one drama to another just lately so let's hope for a busy season when Kayleigh arrives, but without any major incidents.'

'Yes, let's hope so,' Matt said, with a smile. But knowing Elena's uncanny ability to find trouble and his daughter's penchant for drama, he very much doubted it.

Acknowledgements

Thanks to my wonderful husband Allan, to my awesome editor Jill Turner, and to the uber talented Jessica Bell for another fantastic cover. Thanks also to all my lovely friends for their support, especially Su, Julie, Trudy, Tina, Craig, Libby, and Helen.

Thank you for purchasing and reading this book. If you have time to leave a short review so that other readers can find my books, I'd be extremely grateful.

Author's Note

If you enjoyed this you may like the next books in the 'Island Expats' series, coming soon:

    Book 3: Family Matters

    Book 4: to be confirmed

And my other books:

The Island Dog Squad Book 1 (Sandy's Story) Free eBook at this link:
https://dl.bookfunnel.com/wdh6nl8p08

    The Island Dog Squad Book 2 (Another Secret Mission

    The Island Dog Squad Book 3 (People Problems)

    Unlikely Soldiers Book 1 (Civvy to Squaddie)

    Unlikely Soldiers Book 2 (Secrets and Lies)

    Unlikely Soldiers Book 3 (Friends and Revenge)

    Unlikely Soldiers Book 4 (Murder and Mayhem)

    The Afterlife Series Book 1 (Beyond Death) Free eBook at this link:

https://dl.bookfunnel.com/1jaemnpz3d

The Afterlife Series Book 2 (Beyond Life)

The Afterlife Series Book 3 (Beyond Destiny)

The Afterlife Series Book 4 (Beyond Possession)

The Afterlife Series Book 5 (Beyond Limits)

The Afterlife Series Book 6 (Beyond Sunnyfields)

Court Out (A Netball Girls' Drama)

Zak, My Boy Wonder (non-fiction)

And for children:

Jason the Penguin (He's Different)
Jason the Penguin (He Learns to Swim)

Reindeer Dreams

Further information is on my website
https://debmcewansbooksandblogs.com or you can
connect with me on Facebook:
https://www.facebook.com/DebMcEwansbooksandblog
s/?ref=bookmarks

About the Author

Following a career of almost thirty-five years in the British Army, Deb and her husband moved to Cyprus to become weather refugees.

She's written children's books about Jason the penguin and Barry the reindeer and young adult/adult books about dogs, soldiers, and netball players, as well as a non-fiction book about a boy born to be different. Her most popular books are the supernatural suspense Afterlife series which was inspired by ants. Deb was in the garden contemplating whether to squash an irritating ant or to let it live and wondered whether anyone *up there* decides the same about us and thus the series was born.

The first book in the Unlikely Soldiers series is set in nineteen-seventies Britain. The second covers the early eighties and includes the Falklands War, service in Northern Ireland and (the former) West Germany. 'Friends and Revenge' is the third in the series and takes a sinister turn of events. 'Murder and Mayhem' is the final book of the series and takes our heroine from the former West Germany, to London and to an action-packed Hong Kong.

'Court Out (A Netball Girls' Drama)' is a standalone novel. Using netball as an escape from her miserable home life, Marsha Lawson is desperate to keep the past buried and to forge a brighter future. But she's not the only one with secrets. When two players want revenge, a tsunami of emotions is released at a tournament, leaving destruction in its wake. As the wave starts spreading throughout the team, can Marsha and the others escape its deadly grasp, or will their emotional baggage pull them under, with devastating consequences for their families and team-mates?

'Zak, My Boy Wonder', is a non-fiction book co-written with Zak's Mum, Joanne Lythgoe. Deb met Jo and her children when she moved to Cyprus with Allan in 2013. Jo shared her story over a drink one night and Deb was astounded, finding it hard to believe that a family could be treated with such cruelty, indifference and a complete lack of compassion and empathy. This sounded like a tale from Victorian times and not the twenty-first century. When Deb suggested she share her story, Jo said she was too busy looking after both children – especially Zak who still needed a number of surgeries – and didn't have the emotional or physical energy required to dig up the past. Almost fourteen years later, Jo felt ready to share this harrowing but inspirational tale of a woman and her family who refused to give up and were determined not to let the judgemental, nasty, small-minded people grind them down.

'The Island Dog Squad' is a series of novellas inspired by the rescue dog Deb and Allan adopted in 2018. The real Sandy is a sensitive soul, not quite like her fictional namesake, and the other characters are based on Sandy's real-life mates.

Deb loves spending time with her husband Allan and rescue dog Sandy. She also loves writing, keeping fit, and socialising, and does her best to avoid housework.